By the same author

THE COLOUR OF RAIN
THE CRACK
HOTEL DE DREAM
THE BAD SISTER
WILD NIGHTS
ALICE FELL
QUEEN OF STONES
WOMAN BEWARE WOMAN
BLACK MARINA
THE ADVENTURES OF ROBINA

In the 'Cycle of the Sun' series:

THE HOUSE OF HOSPITALITIES
A WEDDING OF COUSINS

For children:

THE SEARCH FOR TREASURE ISLAND
THE GHOST CHILD

A Wedding of Cousins

Emma Tennant

VIKING

VIKING

Published by the Penguin Group
27 Wrights Lane, London W8 5TZ, England
Viking Penguin Inc., 40 West 23rd Street, New York, New York 10010, USA
Penguin Books Australia Ltd, Ringwood, Victoria, Australia
Penguin Books Canada Ltd, 2801 John Street, Markham, Ontario, Canada L3R 1B4
Penguin Books (NZ) Ltd, 182–190 Wairau Road, Auckland 10, New Zealand

Penguin Books Ltd, Registered Offices: Harmondsworth, Middlesex, England

First published 1988

Printed in Great Britain by Richard Clay Ltd, Bungay, Suffolk
Filmset in Monophoto Times

A CIP catalogue record for this book is available from the British Library
ISBN 0-670-81502-0

CHAPTER ONE

Harrods' Bridal Department seemed at first to be more crowded with customers – the about-to-be-wed, the shortly-to-be-in-lawed and the simple gift-buyer – than it actually was. Of these categories, in fact, only the last proved to be entirely genuine, the white-gowned brides and smiling pin-striped escorts turning out to be inanimate mannequins showing off the latest in nuptial wear, while the figure of the 'older man', sometimes of flesh and blood but here and there a model demonstrating tails and grey silk cravat as suitable apparel for the Father of the Bride or Groom, was harder to feel sure of.

With one such type, certainly, there could be little cause for confusion. The lurching and ash-spattered figure of J. D. Hare, father of Amy Rudd's future husband Crispin, was only too clearly the very opposite of an ideal for a Harrods display; while in the case of Lord Lovescombe, the bride's father, an element of doubt maintained right up to the moment of physical contact. Rubbery features and a short, thick-set body, though hardly mandatory for a man playing the part of giving away his daughter, were counterbalanced by a general

1

appearance of immaculate grooming and a fixed, slightly sinister smile which hovered above an oyster silk tie complete with tie-pin of pearl. Conclusive evidence of the reality of this apparition came only when I found myself grasped firmly by the hand.

'Jenny, isn't it?' Lord Lovescombe's smile tried to transform itself into a beam. 'Haven't seen you for ages. You're coming to the wedding of course?'

I had to admit I was surprised at being remembered at all. After the disastrous summer of '53, when Amy's friends, myself among them, had been expelled from Lovegrove following the discovery of her best friend Candida Tarn and Mick Scupper kissing in a Gothic turret in the Children's Garden, four years had passed; and apart from Amy's 'coming-out' ball the year before, in the summer of '56, I had lost touch almost entirely with the Lovescombe family. Despite the pressure of several hundred guests at that event, it seemed that Amy's father had no difficulty in remembering my face; although I had uncomfortably to remind myself that we had bumped into each other on the top landing of his Regent's Park house, while both in search of Amy; and that the circumstances of Amy's discovery had once again involved Mick Scupper, the miscreants this time going further than kissing and even, apparently, going so far as 'all the way'.

Lord Lovescombe continued to wring my hand as we stood there, as if the action would somehow drain us of this unfortunate shared reminiscence. 'I'm surprised to see old Jack Hare up here, I must say,' he said, on a sudden note of resentment. 'Splurging out is definitely not a trait.'

2

Apart from the insinuation that the father of the groom had been less than generous with the distribution of wedding gifts for Crispin, an expression of righteous indignation on Lord Lovescombe's face indicated that some settlement – from the branch of the Azeby family with which J. D. Hare was connected, perhaps – had failed to 'come through'. I had heard, at the fatal Love-grove lunch party just before our expulsion, that a company, Hare, Lovescombe & Rudd, was to be set up at the time of the prospective marriage, providing Crispin with a life in insurance: some recompense for this effort had clearly been anticipated, and, to go by worldly advice on such matters from my Aunt Babs' admirer, the Briga-dier, 'no one likes giving something away for nothing'. The fact that Lord Lovescombe was also about to sur-render his daughter – whether she liked it or not – clearly added to the irritation, suggesting an irresponsible squan-dering of bloodstock as well as capital. More thoughts on this subject were, however, obviated by J. D. Hare's imminent arrival on the scene, his looming figure becom-ing here and there entwined with the white ribbons tradi-tionally attached to a bride's bouquet. The crumpled, baggy suit and shakily clasped extinguished cigarette rapidly eliminated any atmosphere of approaching con-nubial bliss which the department worked so hard to sustain, depicting instead a widower or elderly sufferer of a marriage on the rocks, who spends his waking hours in the pub and sleeps at home in his clothes.

'Came up here to find a gel I said I'd have a drink with.' J. D. Hare blinked at me and then shook his head definitively, as if I had failed in the worst possible way to come up to scratch. 'Carmen . . . you know, that friend

3

of Amy's, Carmen Bye. Said I'd take her to the Bunch of Grapes. And she said something about getting a present for Amy here. Can't think why. It's impossibly dear.'

Before there was an opportunity to get away from the unpleasant effects on Lord Lovescombe of this further proof of the avarice of his daughter's future father-in-law – which I, in my naïvety, considered to be unusual for a writer, imagining a Bohemian expansiveness coming along with the vocation – a *vendeuse* stepped sharply up to the two men. I wondered, as she had probably overheard the remark on the 'dearness' of Harrods, whether J. D. Hare, with his tramp-like appearance, would be asked to leave. Instead, a direction was given out that 'The Honourable Amy Rudd list is at the counter over by the door.'

'I believe there is still a toast-rack available,' Lord Lovescombe said in a tone of irony unfortunately missed by the avant-garde novelist. 'If you're quick,' he added with increased sarcasm.

As Hare looked wildly round for his prey, I considered the implications of this liaison with Carmen. In view of her last involvement, with the painter Bernard Ehrlich, I wondered if she might, unexpectedly after a rebellious school career, decide to become a Muse, necessary to artists for the performance of their holy tasks – and although my last view of her, in the newly fashionable King's Road in Chelsea, had been far from inspiring (Carmen with her sandalled feet and kohl-rimmed eyes, being one of the 'dirty girls' just coming into fashion), there was, as I heard said so often at home with my aunt in her bare, almost spartan North Kensington house, no accounting for tastes. J. D. Hare, admired as he was by such famous arbiters of literary taste as Cyril Connolly and 'Jimbo' Tremlett, editor of the little magazine *Margin*, was possibly suffering from a disease I had heard spoken of, but never successfully analysed, known as writer's block. That Carmen would unblock him at this late stage in his writing life was perhaps his desperate hope.

As we moved towards the door, and to the counter where the bridal lists were watched over by a long-haired girl of Pre-Raphaelite pallor, Carmen herself became visible in the throng.

Apart from a glimpse of Carmen a few days back from the top of the 22 bus as it turned from the King's Road into Sloane Square (where my Aunt Babs had told me to get off and go into Peter Jones to buy some cloth napkins, an unusual request for her and due, as I was later to discover, to the imminent giving of a dinner party to raise money for a charity opera) I had heard nothing of this particular old schoolfriend for some time. The last occasion, I remembered, had been in West London, at the market in Portobello Road. It was on a Saturday morning, when there was just enough of the summer left to light up the aubergines and peppers and corn and give the place a raffish, Caribbean or Mediterranean look before winter set in.

My Aunt Babs was standing at her stall, talking to a group of women who had temporarily abandoned their own 'patch' to exchange pieces of news. Ethel, Aunt Babs' friend who ran a stall for secondhand books and considered herself, perhaps from the long hours of handling authors in their most intimate and battered form, one of the *cognoscenti* of the literary world, closed in on me with an expression of triumph as I made my way through the vegetables and fruit to the area usually referred to as junk.

'Jenny! Just the person I wanted to see.' Ethel, a friend of my family for many years, considered my mother's absence abroad in the cause of my father's job a good excuse for adopting towards me a proprietorial, even wistful air. About sixty years old – which then appeared an age of such magnitude that only H. Rider Haggard, a favourite of mine in my earlier teens but now discarded in favour of Carson McCullers, could have successfully described her – Ethel had taken on the manner and general look of Virginia Woolf. An equine cast of features, straggly bun and protruding gooseberry eyes were complemented by the wearing of long cardigans and thirties brown lace-up shoes, sold at that epoch in the market simply as old shoes rather than antiques. 'Jenny, I know you went to the Lovescombe ball. Tell me – is this by a relative of theirs, do you think? And if so, perhaps you could ask if he has written anything else?'

The slim, grey volume Ethel waved under my nose had a strong, wormy smell and I backed away before taking it: it was reluctantly, too, that I opened the flyleaf to see the title of the book, the lettering on the spine having long ago been washed away by exposure to all weathers (or, possibly, as a glimpse of the words 'Victor Crane', the author's name on the title-page suggested, merely drink). 'Isn't he Lady Lovescombe's brother-in-law?'

The strong fascination felt by the stallholders for the Lovescombe family was, I knew, shared by Ethel. I had, when at St Peter's with Amy, and later after the disastrous summer of the visit to Lovegrove in '53, been an important source of information on the family. Now – disappointingly, to my interlocutors at least (the most pressing of these being my Aunt Babs' friend the Brigadier, who liked to puzzle out the hierarchies of the servants at Lovegrove, the London house in Regent's Park and Castle Azeby, the northern seat) – I had had no news worth imparting since Amy's ball of the year before. Such 'news' as Amy's sudden and ill-advised decision to surrender her virginity on that occasion to Mick Scupper was hardly suitable for proclamation in the market- place.

'I must say I found it an uphill struggle,' Ethel said, indicating the book, now in my hands and obviously intended to stay there, as if we had become somehow caught up in a game of Old Maid. 'It's just that one of my regular customers said Victor Crane was the author of some sort of scandalous novel about the Lovescombe set – which sounded a good deal more enjoyable. She asked me to look out for it actually, and I told her I could go straight to the horse's mouth.'

Ethel, not distant from a horse in appearance herself, let out a high, whinnying laugh as she said this and turned her back sharply before I could return *Memoirs of the Spanish Civil War* by Victor Crane. Apart from the annoyance I inevitably felt when bracketed with a family I hadn't seen for quite a bit, the reminder of the approaching wedding brought only a further onset of anxiety as to what I should wear at the occasion, and even if I should go to it at all.

It was certainly the first I had heard of Victor Crane,

the Communist husband of Lady Lovescombe's sister Mary, being the author of a scandalous novel. This seemed as improbable as being told that a character who is already a scandalous figure in a novel had decided to write one about himself. I told Ethel that I thought his authorship of some kind of *roman-à-clef* improbable; and, given the summer of frustration I had suffered at Ethel's hands a few years back when, giving me holiday reading for a trip with my aunt to the Orkneys, she had pressed the works of George du Maurier into my hands, assuring me that he was responsible for books as compelling as *Rebecca*, I felt myself on firm ground when it came to the inevitable argument.

'Well, never mind,' Ethel finally conceded. A bunch of tourists approached the stalls and the stallholders fell back into place, pushing opaline saucers and silver gilt pepper-pots to the fore, while Ethel, finally relieving me of the *Memoirs of the Spanish Civil War*, shoved it into the 'bargain basket' of books on the pavement. 'What I did enjoy, I do think you would love it, Jenny, is a novel . . . now let me see . . .' Ethel's voice tailed off as one of the tourists lifted a half-jacketed William Sansom from the front of her pile and held it aloft as a method of asking the price.

'No, I don't think you'd enjoy that,' Ethel said with her usual air of literary authority, before turning to me again: 'Yes, I've remembered. *Cheerful Weather for the Wedding* by Julia Strachey. A terribly good novel –'

'Have you anything by Evelyn Woch?' a tourist insisted, lowering *The Office Party* back on the stall. 'Have you *Decline and* . . .?'

'Ah, yes.' Ethel beamed back at him. 'Jenny, dear, just

look in the bag, at the back there. Just got some this morning,' she added as if *Decline and Fall*, and possibly *Scoop* as well, came, like sweets, by the pound. 'I shouldn't be surprised if the wedding at the Loves-combe's is off.' Ethel went on darkly, confusing perhaps her two roles of reader of fiction and gossip-column addict. 'Here we are . . .' She dug into the bag, a sack which had recently contained potatoes and held traces of a particularly sticky black earth. 'Evelyn Waugh. I thought so.'

Rather than watch Ethel exhume the life of Edmund Campion – clearly visible as it rose above the loam – and pass it off on the visitors, I turned and went back to my Aunt Babs and her pile of more easily identifiable goods. It was true, I thought, that Ethel's assumptions this time were likely to be pretty accurate; and I wondered in this case why I hadn't, myself, spotted the probability of Amy's breaking her engagement. The signals, when I had gone four years before to Lovegrove, had been clear enough, Lord Lovescombe talking of some kind of merger between the Hares and the Rudds – the Lovescombe family name – which would provide a salary for young Crispin Hare and a position for Amy as wife and keeper of his house, while Amy had shown a dislike for Crispin that amounted almost to a pathological condition.

It had been the sight, I suppose, of Amy and her brother Ludo together on a sofa in what appeared to be the old schoolroom – a room off a landing on the back stairs at Lovegrove and, unlike the rest of the house, containing books which looked as if they had actually been read – that had deflected me from thoughts of Amy's marriage to her cousin Crispin Hare.

9

When I returned to London after our expulsion from Lovegrove I was too incensed by the injustice of being sent home following the misbehaviour of only one of us, Candida, to ponder much on the plans for Amy's future. I had fallen in love – at least this was the state I had considered myself to be in then, at the age of fourteen – with Ludo, Amy's brother; and was unsure whether the possibly incestuous implications of brother and sister together on a schoolroom sofa were a good thing from my point of view (less likelihood of a rival turning up, with Amy occupying the loved-one's thoughts) or a bad one, in that Ludo would never look elsewhere for happiness when someone as fascinating as Amy would minister to him, like Dorothy Wordsworth and William – or, less happily, Augusta Leigh and Byron.

I had been thrown off course, too, by Amy's absconding at her own ball to the deserted nursery at the top of the Lovescombes' Regent's Park house with Mick Scupper. He it was who had caused our mass exodus from Lovegrove by kissing Candida, though Lady Lovescombe, an energetic *amoureuse* herself, to judge by splashings and other motions in the pond in the Children's Garden with the painter Bernard Ehrlich, had, as Carmen put it at the time, 'nothing to write home about' when it came to virtue or modesty.

These had been the reasons, then, for my surprise at receiving the invitation to Amy's wedding at Castle Azeby in October. Crispin Hare had been displaced from my mind as a future husband for Amy both by Ludo and Mick Scupper. The invitation card indicated therefore that Ethel, more prescient in life than in literature, should at least look at it, hold it to the light and run fingertips over the words, as if a runic reading would in some way decide the odds on the wedding coming off. A dread of the endless discussion of the invitation which was bound to follow my announcement still made me hold back, however, from pulling the stiff, gold-rimmed oblong of cardboard from my coat; and I found myself backing away from Ethel as Aunt Babs now approached from her stall, a tourist having gone off innocently with the life of Edmund Campion.

'It's really quite a nice piece,' Aunt Babs said. 'I suppose it can't be what I think it is?'

These cryptic remarks deflected me from the subject of Amy's wedding – but only, as it turned out, to plunge me back in the Lovescombe family.

This, I admit, was an obsession I had been trying to rid myself of for years, as 'ordinary life' with my Aunt Babs, consisting as it did of learning a trade (I was apprenticed to a friend of hers, a gilder, and earned my keep applying gold leaf to the mirrors and console tables of the residents of Eaton Square) as well as helping with the stall, must be considered superior to the lush and exotic fantasy life led at Lovegrove (and in some kind of tartan version, presumably, at Castle Azeby). I knew very well that Ludo Rudd would in all probability fail to recognize me if we were to come across each other again, he being part of the Lovegrove fantasia, as Aunt Babs drily alluded to the heady weekend of the summer of '53, and not 'the sort of person we know'. I suppose, from the vantage point of the present day, such divisions seem extraordinarily archaic: the glimpse, nevertheless, that I had had of Amy's family had filled me with a restlessness I found hard to sublimate, whether by transferring the

11

state into a continued passion for Ludo – now an ADC to the High Commissioner in Lagos, as Amy had told me on my last fleeting visit to her in Regent's Park – or by owning to myself that I was still curious, and envious too, of the ease of life as personified for me by the Chinese bowl in the hall at Lovegrove; as curious and envious, in some ways, as Ethel might be, or the Brigadier.

It was the memory of the Chinese bowl in the hall at Lovegrove, with its scroll of rampant dragons and sweet-smelling flower petals from a concentrate of summers, that brought to mind again – perhaps on seeing the 'piece' now discussed so eagerly by my aunt and Ethel – the longing I had had to be let in to that way of life, this longing accompanied by a fierce sense of guilt, almost dishonesty. It was as if, by wanting something I could never have, I had already stolen it – yet, as I say, these memories and feelings were probably vastly magnified by the fact that the white china dove now displayed in pride of place on my Aunt Babs' barrow had undeniably been stolen by Carmen in 1953 on the occasion of that weekend visit to Amy's house at Lovegrove.

'It's a Chelsea dove,' Aunt Babs said, 'or I'm completely potty. Ethel, what do you think?'

Before Ethel, who was often asked to pronounce on my Aunt Babs' wares, could make her usual speech on a secondhand copy of *The Spoils of Poynton* being worth more to her than any vulgar object, I asked where the dove had come from, or rather, from whom.

'That's the funny thing,' Aunt Babs said, lapsing into the dreamy voice she unconsciously used when speaking – as a stallholder further down towards the bridge (his name Roly Marr and many of his goods of dubious provenance) was apt to delineate it – of 'bent gear'. 'I do hope it's all right,' Aunt Babs added, her vague, almost trance-like state inducing in me the uneasy sensation that Carmen had, like a goose, just walked over my grave. I felt a sudden chill, thinking of the trouble in store for my poor aunt; and I could see winter come already as it pinched the mangoes and red peppers and turned my Aunt Babs' and Ethel's noses blue.

'Did she – have dark hair?' I stopped, aware of the paucity of language that existed when it came to describing Carmen: to draw her, oddly enough, would have been easier. I thought of a head by da Vinci: hair a Medusa tangle, bulbous lips, eyes with the heavy lids of a stone Gorgon. 'Very curly dark hair,' I amended.

Aunt Babs said she was surprised I could have known this; for reasons of her own, however, she chose not to ask me who I thought the owner of these features could be.

'I think I'd like to buy it,' I said.

Aunt Babs' eyes snapped open, like a cobra which finds the pipe music has stopped and the flute-player's hat has been robbed. 'Certainly not,' she said. 'It's worth more than a year of your wages at the moment, my girl.'

Aunt Babs' descent into music-hall vernacular usually signalled a sense of moral dubiety – with the accompanying implication that only a Victorian discipline would put things straight. 'I'm sure I can think of just the right buyer for it,' she added in a tone implying a do-gooder or philanthropist dedicated to a lifetime spent 'placing' difficult charges. 'He always comes on Saturdays – you used to know him, Jenny. He bought the Watts of *The Moon and Endymion*. I thought it was an

13

absolutely hideous picture, I must say. Henry Azeby sold it to me. They're rather odd, that branch of the family, don't you think?'

The double information imparted by Aunt Babs caused me to thrust my hands nervously into my pockets, and inadvertently I pulled out the invitation, its dull gold gleam attracting Ethel from her stall and catching the eye, collectively, of several other stallholders, accustomed as they were to sifting rubbish for a grain of precious ore. 'Good heavens,' exclaimed Aunt Babs, who was as quick off the mark as any of them. Her hand came out for the card, clashing with Ethel's more rapacious talons as it did so. 'You never told me, Jenny. Well, I must say. At Castle Azeby! And whatever are you going to wear?'

Before I could answer this question, I had (or so it seemed at the time) only a few minutes before deciding what to do about the Chelsea dove. The news that the buyer of the Watts (an erotic study of the moon curving itself about the form of a sensuous-looking Endymion and certainly considered 'hideous' in those days) was returning to examine Aunt Babs' latest spoils – and very probably in the near future, it being Saturday – was extremely agitating. It was Mick Scupper, I knew, who had been the purchaser of the Watts (which later proved to be an excellent investment) and it would be Scupper again who would be offered Amy's uncle's heirloom, and very likely pay a fraction of what it was worth, Aunt Babs' understanding of the real prices going for this type of article being in all likelihood dim. I wondered if he would recognize the bird. It would be too much of a gamble, certainly, to wait until it was in his hands and then blurt out its provenance; and besides that, I had no idea whether I should say that Carmen had stolen it from the Orphic groves of Amy's 'Uncle Si', the dove being a leftover from the collection of his mother, Marguerite, Lady Azeby; or whether the imputation of receivership of stolen goods might land Aunt Babs in the clink. It was also necessary to bear in mind that Scupper would be unlikely to wish to be reminded of the weekend in the summer of '53 when his kissing of Candida Tarn at Lovegrove had had us expelled – 'thrown out of the garden of Eden', as the Brigadier had remarked with some relish at the time. Scupper's own conduct, that of attempting to seduce a minor, might well have been illegal, his standing with the police possibly a tenuous one and as little in need of investigation as some of the hopeful vendors who brought their bits and pieces to the stall.

I decided, with a good deal of anguish, to keep quiet. The decision was helped by the unwelcome appearance of Scupper himself at the far end of the market, where expensive antiques give over to stalls of bananas and cabbages. Here the stalls form a barrier difficult to negotiate on market day for a good stretch of the road before the start of the old clothes and junk.

Part of the reason for my decision lay with the mention of Henry Azeby, provider of the Watts to Aunt Babs and thus supplier of Scupper with the basis for his much ridiculed, but subsequently vastly valuable, collection of Victorian oils. Henry Azeby, of whom I had heard news only occasionally from Amy, was spoken of by his cousin with derision, she going so far as to say that Henry had no right to help himself to the heirlooms at his father's mansion, somewhere near (apparently) Castle Azeby; that his father was 'on to him' and had threatened to prosecute if any more of these artefacts vanished; and that unscrupulous dealers, only too happy to provide young Azeby with the wherewithal for another evening of debauch, should be reported if they were seen to be displaying the goods. Not wanting Aunt Babs, innocent of all this and interested only in proclaiming that she never read the gossip columns in which Henry Azeby was reported in his cavortings with minor royalty, to become, despite herself, a handler of stolen goods, soon to be known throughout the trade as a 'fence', I came to the conclusion that the less she knew of the origins of the white china dove, the less likely was she to blurt out something under interrogation. I resolved, too, that I would rescue the dove and return it to its rightful owner – though whether 'Uncle Si', in one of his afternoon sleeps in the hammock in the woods at Lovegrove, might simply have considered the dove to have flown home of its own accord, was a matter difficult to decide.

I had first met Mick Scupper on the banks of the River Avon, on the day Candida arrived for her longed-for visit to Lovegrove. The day was memorable not only for being the reason of our disembarkation from Cythera (or so I fancifully saw it, forced to spend the rest of the holidays trailing the National Gallery with Daniel Stringer, offspring of friends of Aunt Babs – all Renaissance depictions of a lush Eden being painful and forcible reminders of Lovegrove), but also because it was the occasion of Candida's turning so dramatically the other way and substituting her passion for Amy with an even stronger one for Scupper. The results had been disastrous; but apart from the obvious cooling between Amy and her self-appointed best friend, there had, it appeared, been a continuing rivalry, its culmination taking place at Amy's ball in an act of love – if so it could be called where Mick Scupper was concerned, his blondness and cold blueness of eye only too correctly proclaiming a ruthless and manipulative character. I wondered if Candida had known of Amy's seduction at the ball; and whether, if she had known, she had minded. My most powerful memories of her on that occasion were of a stiff, dancing figure, endlessly fox-trotting with some young man presumably produced by Lady Lovescombe for the purpose. Candida's brother Leo, who, Amy told me, had at first sent a rude refusal to the dance, had in the end decided to come, to see 'the last bastions of feudalism' (his appellation) in 'their death throes'. All this had been confided to me as I stood, acting the part of wallflower which Ethel had only too accurately predicted for me, and thus grateful to seem to be in conversation with anyone, even if that person was Leopold Tarn.

That the Lovescombe family were far from their death throes was amply borne out by the abundance of champagne, a profusion of red roses, and a marquee rumoured to have cost several thousand pounds to erect. For Leo, who three years before, in the throes of infatuation for Carmen, had had his car towed away from the Lovescombes' ball for their son Ludo, this must have been a triumphant occasion, giving an opportunity both to insult his hosts and to revel in their hospitality.

Now, standing for want of anywhere else at his side, I wondered how, on that midsummer's night in '53, I had found Candida's brother so attractive and fascinating. I was too young then, I suppose, to be able to see the characteristics which would later, when Leo's fatal attachment to Amy brought her into the world of radical politics and himself into a world known to himself and his friends as 'philistine and bourgeois', come to be described by various enemies within his own faction as 'Stalinist'. I would certainly sense his arrogance, first noted as a habit of banging a broom on the floor of his room as a demand for service from his mother or sister (this demand always satisfied immediately by the rushing up of food – 'Too killing! Things called bratwurst or pumpernickel', as Lady Lovescombe, with her usual sweeping ignorance, would remark in one of her short-lived questionings with Amy, on the subject of the comic German food at the Tarns').

At Amy's ball, Leo's roving eye, slouching posture and faintly sardonic grin had suggested an increase in this arrogance, the fact of our being joined together for the simple reason that we knew nobody else obviously seeming offensive to him, while as far as I was concerned the ass's head of Leo's last, doomed fixation for Carmen was clearly visible, causing further embarrassing ruminations on the nature of love, fantasy and reality. I had, it was true, met and 'fallen for' Ludo rather than Leo since that night, but it was patently clear that some sort of philtre would be needed to make me even recognizable to Amy's brother on this occasion. For all that, I looked round the dance-floor eagerly for a glimpse of either of them. Leo, also scanning the sea of dancers with desperation, suddenly shouted out and pointed a finger at a man lurching at the side of the dance-floor, his gait that of a riderless horse unsure of whether it is still a part of the race.

'Isn't that Victor Crane?' Leo's voice rose to a high

pitch against the music of Paul Adams and his band, by now producing such hits of the time as 'Something's Gotta Give' and 'Cherry Pink and Apple Blossom White' at full blast. 'He used to edit *Seventh Day*.' Admiration on Leo's part was evident over the sound of the music. 'You've met him, haven't you Jenny? Go and bring him over here.'

This new command took me back to the evening of my arrival at Lovegrove, and my first 'grown-up' dinner party, a memory which still fills me with shame and horror, as if some crime had been perpetrated then, and I was the only one who could supply the missing clues – although it was hard to say whether 'bringing in' Victor Crane to dinner had really been the cause of the disastrous sequence of events which followed. Crane was certainly not someone I wanted to bring anywhere, after witnessing the results of my late arrival in the dining-room at Lovegrove in his company. His lolling head, like the head of Holofernes grasped by Judith, had seemed by some optical illusion to be held in the pale and delicate hands of Marguerite, Lady Azeby, whose full-length portrait in white chiffon was positioned exactly behind him. Clearly there had been a connection between Crane's non-co-operation with the soup – unless a fully facial immersion in the stuff could be considered a token of enthusiasm – and the subsequent spillage of the entire grouse platter down the necks of Crane's wife Mary and her neighbour, the water-colourist Walter Neet. A flustered passage of bread sauce and gravy between Vine, the butler, and the parlourmaid had done little to improve matters; and over the intervening years I had often wondered whether I had done the wrong thing in bring-

19

ing Crane in: whether it wasn't taken for granted, even, that he should be left behind, among the debris of the pre-dinner drinks and 'cleared up' with them, by the staff: that I had, in fact, committed my first major solecism in the eyes of Lady Lovescombe, earning a black mark which, added to the misdemeanour the next day of Candida and Mick Scupper, would lead inevitably to our being sent away. None of these reflections, however, stood in the way of Victor Crane, who spotted me and gave a baffled frown, clearly deciding to come over on his own – unaided and with an ambling gait that caused two dancing couples to collide.

'I know where it was!' Crane peered at me as if I were some forgotten stag party, the empty glasses of which remain perplexingly the morning after in one's room. 'It was at Lovegrove!'

'The last bastion of feudalism!' Leopold Tarn seized this opportunity to step forward and introduce himself. 'I'm a great admirer of yours,' he added quickly, as Crane shuffled uncertainly on the spot. '*Seventh Day*. We're starting up something similar ourselves, at Oxford.'

'Name the evil man,' Crane suddenly shouted in a lull in the music, a mild consternation starting up at this trumpeted call. 'That was a bloody good column, wasn't it? Oh, we exposed some of those Fascist moneybags, all right, didn't we? Mind you, it's not the thirties nowadays ... but you've still got your villains today ... and I don't mind saying there are a few here tonight.' Crane's burst of laughter, succeeded by an acute coughing fit, was the probable cause of the start of a hasty rendering of 'La Vie en Rose', the tune itself seeming to produce, like fairies in a pantomine, the spectacle of Lady Lovescombe and her sister Mary Crane as they made their way purposefully in our direction. As if subliminally aware of this, Crane pulled himself up to his full height and, addressing Leopold Tarn with solemnity, continued his harangue with as much volume as he could muster.

'There's no doubt that what Nasser did today was absolutely right. The canal belongs to Egypt. The sooner the imperialists in this country realize it, the better. Nationalize the Suez Canal! Absolutely right! As I said at dinner to Richard Lovescombe, who is, as you might imagine . . .'

Efforts to alert Crane to the arrival of his wife and hostess being of no avail, I tried signalling to Leo, who was himself in the disadvantaged position of having been briefly expelled by one and having never met the other; and this attempt being equally hopeless, found to my unexpected relief that Carmen, in the mass of people ('right-wing politicians, titled Bohemia', as Leo had growled at me earlier), had become suddenly visible. A substantial number of people had gone down for the ball supper ('Bring back the menu' had been Aunt Babs' urgent instruction, a lively dispute having broken out between herself and the Brigadier as to whether a full meal, with galantine of ham, salmon mayonnaise and strawberry meringue would be served, or a simple kedgeree). Carmen in turn saw me and beckoned to me forcefully to come over.

'Lovescombe is a full-fledged reactionary,' Crane roared, as Lady Lovescombe and her sister reached his side and fixed icy stares on Leopold Tarn (and indeed on me, as I beat a path over to Carmen). 'Put Nasser up against the wall and shoot him! That's his point of view! Capitalist swine!'

'Victor, please!' Mary Crane's voice was soon lost in the roar of the ball; and, hardly daring to look round to see if Lady Lovescombe's displeasure was also vented on Leo – perhaps, like royalty, she 'never forgot a face' and remembered the 'prang' at Ludo's ball between Leo's old Morris and the royal Daimler (or perhaps, like many from all walks of British life, she never forgot anything concerning royalty) – I took Carmen's outstretched hand and gladly let myself be pulled out of the ballroom and down to a small half-landing study evidently used by the Lovescombes for the occasional viewing of television.

CHAPTER TWO

It is possible, I suppose, to see the evening of Amy's ball in Regent's Park as a kind of signpost: one which led, after directions to a false destination (in this case to her wedding a year later) to the new age; and that like those country crossroads where at different junctions the same place is advertised, but, despite the closeness to each other of the farmsteads or villages, the place itself is shown at wildly fluctuating distances, it would have been virtually impossible then to pick out the most probable route to the future.

There was no doubt, however, that certain seeds of the times that lay, on that evening in July 1956, unimaginably far away at the opening of the next decade, could have been discernible to someone cleverer – and older – than myself. I saw only the first manifestations of the casual violence which was to be taken for granted before long; and, too, the first signs of the craze for personal publicity – an element of modern life at first deplored by the Lovescombes – which was equally to overtake society, turning people and things alike into saleable commodities and promoting money before all else, so that those values, however easily ridiculed, of the Brigadier, say, or of Aunt Babs herself, with her dedication to art and frugal pleasures, were totally swept away. That the Loves-combes had no desire for their worth, their 'holdings', or, as Victor Crane quaintly put it, 'the quantity of their spondulicks', to be made known to the world at large was hardly surprising: they had as little control, however, of the coming boom in advertising and vulgar journalism as anyone else; and soon 'opened' Lovegrove, ostensibly for reasons of financial survival, but in fact in order to join the new fashion for being photographed on one's lawn in the just-arrived colour magazine features of the time. And, significantly enough, it was their nephew Henry Azeby, at the time of Amy's ball about twenty-one years old, who led the way (his friendship with Scupper, forged that night and little harmed very probably by the discovery a year later that Scupper had bought the Watts of *The Moon and Endymion* through the intermediary of Aunt Babs, thus paying less than if he had been offered the picture outright) which led me away from understanding what was really going on. For, surely, people so close to the family could hardly be anything other than disinterested; and if Scupper and Henry Azeby then showed themselves as the profiteers and the publicists of the coming age, it was at that moment almost impossible to spot, just as much as the fact that Amy was their helpless prey.

Thoughts of Amy – as I had glimpsed her so far at her ball: white, fluttering in a white dress, with movements as far distant from her striding, swooping walk at Love-grove as those of an eagle from a dove – made me think of Carmen's theft, at 'Uncle Si's', of the white china bird so nearly dropped on the river bank, but still, presumably, safe in Carmen's keeping. Knowing that this was hardly the best moment to approach her – to offend Carmen would very likely result in remaining friendless for the rest of the evening – I decided anyway to ask her about it. Stolen goods were, after all, a serious matter: no one knew this better than I, given Aunt Babs' extreme fear of being their innocent handler. (Roly Marr, the dealer under the bridge in Portobello Road, who, on his way to becoming the most famous *antiquaire* and decorator of the approaching years of conspicuous consumption, was also a walking encyclopaedia on the provenance of nearly every piece offered to Aunt Babs, would have had no difficulty in identifying the piece.) And it seemed best, as far as I could see, to warn Carmen of the possible consequences of her crime. That the thing would turn up the following year on my aunt's stall I could hardly of course have known – but it was with a sort of prescient chill that I plunged into the subject, despite her recent rescue of me from the clutches of Victor Crane and Leo, his new disciple. Beside the need to express moral outrage (a need of which I was cured, later, by the perception of my own fabrications, particularly when it came to the attempt to secure Ludo for myself) there was also the desire, strong in self-satisfied people, to 'know more' about the miscreant they have chosen to persecute. Carmen, dressed unusually for a coming-out ball in a black polo-neck jersey and what appeared to be skiing slacks, seemed at first delighted by my inter- rogation, as if it amounted to no more than an exchange of 'news' between old friends who have seen little of each other since school.

'Of course I wasn't asked!' Carmen's eyes glittered in a way that was indeed horribly reminiscent of St Peter's, the occasion of her impersonation of Lady Pickering, one of the school Governors, coming to mind. Mention of the dove became inadvisable. This time, furthermore, her eyes, famously black – a sign according to her of exotic lineage (gypsy, Eastern potentate or whatever Carmen had decided on at the time) – were lined with kohl, a 'look' which was making its way irrevocably from Chelsea to the rest of the world, but which was still considered, at that time, *outré*; and in Carmen's case particularly so, the kohl adding to the general impression of a Muslim princess. 'No, it was easy enough for me to get in,' Carmen said. 'I came with Johnny Bouzouki and "Bluey" Stavrakis.' Seeing that this news left me cold, she yawned loudly and continued as if addressing a hopelessly backward pupil. 'For God's sake, Jenny. The shipping fortune. Even you have presumably read about Bluey's three-masted schooner.'

I had to admit I hadn't. If the (concealed) interests of my Aunt Babs might go as far as the Lovescombe family, they certainly didn't extend to Greek shipping magnates, who, if mentioned at all, would probably be held up as examples of the despoliation of that ancient land since the days of Homer and the arrival of goats. I replied to Carmen that the three-masted schooner sounded very lovely, and asked if she had been on board. Carmen spluttered with amusement. 'We cruised the Aegean in June. It was heaven. There's a Toulouse-Lautrec in the main saloon.'

Before I could digest this information any further, a slight tearing sound in the doorway announced the presence of a net dress – most of the dresses at the ball, indeed, were made of this material, some with artificial roses attached and others plain; some pink, and many white – in this case a white one apparently having snagged itself against the study door. A faint, sibilant sigh came from the invisible wearer.

'Johnny and Bluey thought they'd do some of the London season before going up to Scotland,' Carmen continued, 'and of course nothing could be easier than getting in here.'

'Why's that?' I remembered the presence of Vine, the Lovescombes' butler, at the door – a Cerberus who I hoped hadn't received any harmful treatment from Bouzouki and Co. – though the very thought of the mild English tenor of the evening being disturbed by hoodlum behaviour seemed so improbable as to be fanciful, Vine simply being there to receive the cards of the guests and to ask those gossip columnists who had hoped to don black tie and gain admittance to return whence they came. A faint prescient coldness, as I say, visited me that evening, however, and my heart sank when Carmen gave her famous 'wicked' grin. 'My dear Jenny, you still are a little baby, aren't you? Lord Lovescombe wouldn't dare not to admit Bluey to his party. Do I have to spell out why? Still living in never-never-land with that made-up aunt, aren't you?'

I don't know which of Carmen's accusations annoyed me more: that I had stayed a child whilst her immoral cruises – as Aunt Babs would doubtless see them – had gained her automatic entry to the world of mature decisions and responsibility; or that Aunt Babs had in some way been invented by me, the latter charge being particularly galling when Carmen had 'made up' enough parents to people a colony, the most recent, if I remembered correctly, being no less than King Zog of Albania. 'No,' Carmen went on before I had time to answer, 'Bluey's got something "on" poor old Amy's dad, I can tell you.'

The cough which now broke out behind us, while belonging to the wearer of the snagged – but now freed – white net dress, could also only have belonged to one person; and I looked round more quickly than Carmen, she being still immersed in the start of her tale of City corruption and gangland blackmail procedures. Candida stood before us, her face almost the colour of the just-torn dress: her manner, however, showing that it was damage to the Lovescombe family reputation rather than to her frock that had turned her pale.

'Good evening, Carmen.' The voice, like a dry, over-prim cough which has been repressed over hours of school concerts or prize-givings and only released at a convenient moment, took me at a speed I hardly desired to the evening when Carmen, playing her cruellest trick on Candida, had announced us all invited to Ludo's ball at this very house. The clipped, dismissive tone, unsuitable, as it proved, at the time, was also reminiscent of the way Candida had replied to the police constable's queries on our arrest in a midnight attempt to reach Regent's Park and the ball on foot; the arrest having been more or less inevitable, given that Candida had insisted on wearing her school hat for the expedition, this especially causing our instant return to the Tarn household.

'And what has Mr Bluey Stavrakis got "on" Lord Lovescombe, I'd like to know?'

It was clear from Candida's tone that she, at least, had grown up a lot since the days when an invitation to Lovegrove had been the only way of learning the ways of the world – as it had been, indeed, for all of us. Candida, it could be said, had learnt them only too quickly and forced our expulsion by her quick agreement to go off to the Children's Garden with Mick Scupper. Now I wondered if it was Scupper's continued attentions which had educated Candida to the existence of such people as 'Bluey' Stavrakis. The young auctioneer was, I knew, presently operating at Christie's and was probably dispatched regularly to the Aegean in order to value the Toulouse-Lautrecs and other masterpieces. The thought crossed my mind – though it was certainly, as Ethel would have put it, too 'boggling' to consider seriously – that Candida had even been on the same cruise as Carmen, a contrast indeed from the days of St Peter's when Carmen's continual boasting of French and American boyfriends had been a world away from Candida's pigeon-chested and Aertex-shirted devotion to Amy Rudd and no one else. These possibilities were soon dismissed, however, by the appearance of Scupper himself at the door to the study, an effete and highly coloured young man in attendance: behind them both, but securely attached by the hand, stood Amy.

'There's been share-tipping going on.' Carmen was in the midst of a speech, almost incomprehensible as far as I was concerned, but for all I knew easily understood by Candida (who had, I had heard, got into Oxford from St Peter's without any difficulty), on the subject of Lord Lovescombe's irregular connections in Threadneedle Street. 'He didn't have any control over what happened to Hare, Lovescombe & Rudd,' Carmen went on, as the trio in the doorway, recognizing the name, began to walk in; 'but that's not going to bother Johnny and Bluey. No sirree. It was as much as I could do, I can assure you, to stop them from calling in the boys and roughing old Lovers up.'

I don't know whether Candida or Amy moved first, to put an end to this highly embarrassing exposé of the underworld dealings of Greeks and (if she was to be believed) honest English City gents: that it wasn't myself is certain, for the combination of the destruction of a mental picture – held at that time, I believe, by almost everyone in post-war England – of furled umbrellas, brief-cases and probity, the City a sort of continuation of 'running the country' in the war, something which even my Aunt Babs, a seasoned Churchill-hater, had had to admit the leader had been able to do – combined, as I say, with the unpleasant tone of boastful violence on Carmen's part, was enough to keep me rooted to the spot. As if sensing impending revolt from the direction of the study door, she swung round and directed a beam-ing smile at Amy and her companions.

'Amy! I know you don't mind me breaking in like this.' I was uncomfortably aware, as Carmen spoke, of the occasion of the theft of the Chelsea dove, and of Carmen's odd implication that the ornament was in some way common property. 'The thing is, I've got some friends – Bluey Stavrakis and Johnny Bouzouki – listen to this. Amy, it's so priceless . . . they're gun-dogs of your father's.'

'Gun-dogs?' Amy's eyes were suddenly reminiscent of her mother's, Lady Lovescombe's cold blue orbs being famed for the ability to repel a bounder at five hundred yards. For a second I felt a twinge of pity for Carmen, as Amy's eyes next raked the black polo-neck and slacks; but that Candida felt no such emotion was evident from the way in which she stepped into the middle of the room – between, so to speak, the devil and the deep-blue sea. She held out her arms imploringly, this also horribly memory-provoking of the St Peter's production of *Hamlet*, in which Amy had (as the Brigadier, himself in the audience with Aunt Babs for the occasion, commented) 'wowed them' with the length and shapeliness of her legs in black tights, while Candida, adoring, had played Laertes.

'Please, Carmen.' Candida's elocution lessons, at least, had proved as unrewarding as the teacher had predicted at the time, writing, if I remember rightly, to Mrs Tarn and suggesting Candida's removal from class, both to obviate unnecessary expense and to save the professional's reputation when it came to failing a Gold Medal for Speech. The flat, tinny tones produced a frown on Amy's face; while I, still unsure of what to make of anything going on round me, stayed as motionless as before. The thought crossed my mind that Amy's frown was caused by the presence of Candida, once Amy's rival for the affections of Mick Scupper and, for all I knew, the art expert's girlfriend to this day. Scupper, certainly, showed no sign of embarrassment at the proximity of Amy and Candida: he even, it occurred to me, failed to recognize Candida altogether, which, in the never-never-land to which Carmen had perhaps accurately consigned me, seemed extraordinary in view of the 'heavy petting' reported by the Lovescombe governess Miss Bolton on the occasion of the last, fatal lunch at Lovegrove.

Amy's presence was only too evidently known to Scupper. His hand was round her wrist, giving her the air of a prisoner, captured suddenly in flowing gown and about to be taken off to the Tower (though whether it was my overheated imagination which had returned me to the turret in the Children's Garden at Lovegrove, scene of Candida's betrayal of Amy, that suggested Amy's destination I don't know). The idea that Amy was enjoying her chained status – that she was in perfect control of her situation, even – came to me when she replied to Carmen, her tone as measured and resonant as poor Candida's, her defender's, had been strained and unconvincing.

'Bluey and Johnny are old friends of Daddy's. Of course they were asked,' she said. The slight inflection on the word 'they' would have caused a more sensitive person than Carmen to wince; and this Candida patently did, though she had, this time at least, undoubtedly received an invitation to the ball. 'But how very nice to see you, Carmen,' Amy went on at her most glacial. 'I do hope you're enjoying yourself.'

'Oh for God's sake, Amy, don't be so pompous! I was only trying to tell you a joke – the Greeks say "gun-dog" when they're trying to say "contact" – that's all. They're "gun-dogs" of your father's – that's honestly all I was saying!'

It was hard to like Amy at that moment. It occurred to me later – in view of her subsequent unexpected, even eccentric behaviour – that she had been quite unhappy for a long time: that she had been 'frozen' somehow, in the world's expectations of her and, more specifically, in the mould prepared for her by the Lovescombes for her future life. Having left St Peter's immediately after

School Cert (in which examination, Candida told me the following term, when the school was conspicuously empty of Amy's baffling, sometimes infuriating presence, she had failed maths and Latin), a desultory education followed, similar to the hotch-potch of French, drawing and music lessons forced on young ladies at the time of Jane Austen; and, as with Jane Austen's heroines, there was then to be a season – not too many of these, it was to be hoped – and after that, marriage. Now was her only opportunity for adventure – a reluctant recognition of which might account for the icy disdain to those who, like Carmen, had a more free and reckless attitude to life. At the time, I must admit, I felt only an instinctive revulsion to Amy, going so far as to hope, even, that Candida had scored several points over her old idol when it came to the conquest of Scupper. But these thoughts, and any other childish considerations, were soon put out of mind by Scupper's own flamboyant gestures, which, accompanied by Henry Azeby's florid face – this appearing to jig about on the end of an immensely tall neck, like a technicolored giraffe – lent a sudden circusring atmosphere to the ball staircase and the study, the former becoming, as Scupper waved and called, blocked by guests brought to a standstill by his actions; among these being J. D. Hare and his wife and son, Crispin.

'Ladees and Gentlemen!' Scupper's ringside imitation, embarrassing in the extreme, received hoots of delighted laughter from Henry Azeby – at that stage in his life newly out of some sort of expensive remand centre, or so according to Ethel, who had found the information in a newspaper too low even for the wrapping of the newly fashionable opaline wares in which Aunt Babs had begun to specialize. 'Roll up! See the lady show the Vandykes. Two shillings and sixpence pleess!'

As Scupper's handsome face ('He looks like a barrowboy' was to be the Brigadier's comment some years later at the time of the first wave of publicity garnered for Scupper by himself, with the simultaneous acquisition of *Man Ahoy!* magazine and his election as Conservative MP for Great Yarmouth) retreated with Amy in the direction of the downstairs rooms, Carmen, feeling perhaps my sudden sympathy, turned and grinned up at me from the chair in which she had had the composure to remain throughout Amy's dismissive greeting. 'Ridiculous, isn't it? I must say, I've never heard such a load of balls in my life!'

Despite another feeling of revulsion, brought about very probably by my provincial upbringing, I asked Carmen whether she meant it was untrue that Bluey and Johnny were in fact friends of Lord Lovescombe; or whether she would stick to her story of mafioso violence and blackmail.

'That's not the point.' As so often with Carmen, the interest value for her of one of her tales lasted for considerably less time than that of her hearers. 'No – it's that idiot Mick Scupper. He's got her round his little finger. Couldn't you see?'

The simile was uncomfortably apt, particularly in view of the manipulative hold on Amy's wrist which Scupper had chosen to maintain, as if the puppet's strings could more easily be managed from this angle. I remembered the sketches of Scupper in the 'rough' books of both Candida and Amy at St Peter's, pages of the coarse-grained paper intended for the trying-out of algebraic formulae dedicated to the famous triangular face and quiff of hair; and I felt less surprise that a girl as obviously intelligent as Amy should fail her maths exam. (Candida, it went without saying, would have been coached and cajoled by Dr and Mrs Tarn, or perhaps wouldn't have needed the incentives, her sense of self-perfection dictating the simultaneous conduct of a stormy, under-age love-affair with the sitting of papers in many subjects.)

'Is Candida still . . . I mean, going on dates with . . .?'

Carmen laughed loudly, causing Crispin Hare, about to enter the room with the sort of stealthy assurance adopted by a self-conscious guest at the ball of a powerful older relative, to back out again at speed. 'No, no. Candida's got bigger fish to fry.' And, as I came closer to her – while aware at the same time of a bubble of amusement breaking out on the stairs, and a roar of shouting and applause from below – Carmen went on, 'I thought you'd know that Jenny, of all people. But I suppose you're all wrapped up in that arty little world of yours. No –' And here – as I felt my heart flutter, and fought against the insinuations in Carmen's voice, determining to return to the ballroom if only to find Leo and Victor Crane still in their, so to speak, revolutionary positions – Carmen rose and came up to mutter with a breath that smelt strongly of red wine, 'No, Jenny, one has to feel sorry for Crispin Hare! I mean, the poor boy is a total virgin!'

Carmen's information, as so often, was unnecessary and vaguely disgusting. She came over and slapped me heartily on the back, as if we were two clubland men who had just exchanged a joke that would be described by Ethel as 'decidedly risqué', or by the Brigadier as plain 'blue'. 'I work as a hostess in the clubs when I need a bob or three,' Carmen said. 'The Stork's the best, every-one's so pissed they buy you a bottle of champagne and don't even bother to see if you drink it. Anyway, poor old Crispin came in last week.'

'Carmen, I'm not sure you should . . .'

'You're not sure! I can tell you, dearie, he wasn't one bit sure either.' Carmen let out a bellow of laughter. I began to feel uneasy. Candida had vanished downstairs in the wake of Scupper and Amy, and a growing sense of anxiety came over me that her 'bigger fish to fry' might indeed be the 'son of the house', as Ethel, steeped in her pulp romances, would inevitably refer to Ludo. I decided to leave Carmen before the deflowering of Crispin Hare could be described in full detail, only reflecting on poor Amy's low chances of happiness (if she were indeed to marry her cousin) by the time I reached the door. Carmen must have read my thoughts, for she called out, 'That's what all the row was about, see. Old Pa Lovescombe sold out young Hare's share to Bluey. Without telling the budding insurance broker, or indeed his father, the eminent novelist.'

'What on earth do you mean?' I remembered transac-tions of one kind or another going on at the lunch before our dismissal from Lovegrove – transactions which ap-peared to suggest some merger between the Lovescombes and the Hares. The memory of the queue for roast beef in the great Edwardian dining-room, and Victor Crane's placing of his hand palm down in a dish of horseradish, rose irresistibly to mind, as did the extreme discomfort, endured alone, of knowing that the dove stolen by Carmen was all the time in her 'bucket bag', dangling from one of the chairs at the main table. These successive thoughts stopped me in my tracks, a sense of duty instilled by Aunt Babs telling me that I must confront Carmen with her theft even at this distance of years.

'It's Lovescombe, Stavrakis & Rudd now.' Carmen's mind-reading had evidently come to a halt some way before the disastrous summer visit to the Lovescombes' southern seat. 'Bluey decided he'd take the old family firm in lieu of payment for Lovers' debts and he got in there for free. Just like tonight!'

'Carmen –' A round of applause from downstairs distracted me for a moment and Carmen, pushing me aside, swept out of the room ahead of me. 'They'll patch it up somehow,' she threw back over her shoulder. 'Crispin's the heir at umpteen removes to the other Azeby place, since young Henry got disinherited by his pa. Amy and Crispin together would roll the two estates into one – see?'

With this Carmen had gone – not downstairs, as I had assumed she would, but up a handful of stairs to the entrance to the ballroom, her sense of timing proving as dangerous but exact as ever, as both J. D. Hare and Victor Crane, the former now separated from his family, descended in search – or so J. D. Hare could be heard to mutter – of 'more serious refreshment'.

'My dear . . . Jenny! An example to the young Communists!' Victor Crane was proud, perhaps, of having the acquaintance of a member of the younger generation, and keen to show J. D. Hare that he, unlike the experimental writer, had a shrewd sense of what was going on in the present. That this was the case I could only surmise much later; at the time Crane's insistence on our long-standing connection was baffling in the extreme, particularly given the unfortunate circumstances of our last meeting, when my 'bringing him in' to dinner at Lovegrove had resulted, on his part, in a near coma for the rest of the evening. That I was a 'young Communist' was also certainly a fabrication and must have accounted for my incredulous expression at Crane's introduction of me in this guise to the father of Crispin Hare.

'Communist, eh?' J. D. Hare swept me with his eyes; then, noting that the presence of himself and Crane made it impossible for me to get out of the room, chuckled in a way that could only be described as malevolent. It occurred to me that the time I was having at the ball, so far, for all the glories of the marquee, the pink-lit chandeliers and gold chairs crowded about tables each with its champagne bucket and spray of moss roses, was not going to provide the sort of 'copy' expected by the Brigadier and Ethel – and, surreptitiously, Aunt Babs. Ethel would not be so pleased to hear of the presence of the avant-garde novelist, despite her trade as bookseller, when tales of heirs and tiaras were in order; and Victor Crane, despite his close kinship with the hostess, could be of little interest to her on such an occasion. That I was trapped, however, was becoming desperately clear to me, particularly as J. D. Hare's lips, which bore a greenish sludge at the corners, approached my hair and attempted to whisper a confidence. Inaudible because of the din, he continued to mutter in a never-ending sibilant flow – conceivably the 'stream of consciousness' alluded to by Jim Tremlett, editor of *Margin* and so-despised husband of Jasmine (though whether the tension between the couple at that distant weekend at Lovegrove had been due to another 'stream' emanating from Lord Lovescombe and received by Jasmine Tremlett on the occasion of their assignations in the Chinese garden, I could never know).

'What I simply cannot understand,' roared Crane, 'is why Donald and Guy haven't been in touch for such ages! I mean, I simply haven't had my marching orders at all!'

I'd heard from Amy, on a long, grey afternoon when we'd had a chance to meet between her Florentine art courses and my apprenticeship at the gilding shop, that Victor Crane – just glimpsed weaving his way down Regent's Park Road in search of a pub, after a probably 'dry' visit to Lady Lovescombe – was, in his own view at least, the 'Third Man' of the Burgess and MacLean scandal and particularly aggrieved at that time that no one was interested to hear it. Now, maddened by the obduracy of J. D. Hare, combined with the writer's intended intimacy with a young woman, Crane lurched forward and delivered a kick to the novelist's behind, an action which sent both men sprawling. The study door, closed by Hare while attempting to open the cabinet where Lord Lovescombe kept his malt whisky and silver-tagged carafes of gin and brandy, now opened sharply. Lady Lovescombe stood face to face with me – as she had done, I remembered without any cheer, on the evening at Lovegrove when she had insisted on Ludo's playing cards and had mistaken me for Candida.

'Good evening, Jenny!' There seemed little doubt now in her mind as to who I was; and, unfairly – unless you can count a state of consciousness as the badge of moral responsibility – whom she considered to blame for the shambles in the room caused by the fallen and, in Crane's case, heavily snoring men.

'I'm so sorry, Lady Lovescombe.' I felt that this time I could reasonably have been mistaken for Candida – both prim and deferential – even though I was on this occasion identified as being myself. 'Everyone just bumped . . . into each other,' I went on lamely.

'So I see.' Lady Lovescombe stretched out an arm in the direction of the staircase. An index finger pointed to the way down, while other fingers, stiff with aquamarines and diamonds, seemed to reflect the hard light in her eyes. 'Go and get Vine at once, please.'

'Yes, Lady Lovescombe.' I stepped with feelings of extreme trepidation over J. D. Hare, in order to get through the door: apparently 'out for the count' (as the Brigadier, himself a heavy drinker, was to remark later with relish) Hare might be: yet he was well capable of springing to the attack. Of the two fallen men, Crane was the more defenceless so that it was difficult to conjecture how long, as a member of British Intelligence (if such he was), he would be able to last at the hands of the KGB. Hare, undeterred, it seemed, by finding himself in a supine position, now revived again and continued his fast, excited muttering, while I made my way to the door as unostentatiously as I could.

'Get up at once, Jack!'

'Abso-lutely – Anne. Too awful. Must have slipped!' Hare's voice, now that an urgent state of affairs had announced itself, changed rapidly from sibylline whisperings to an oracular, almost sepulchral tone. This, I saw, could have been on account of Lord Lovescombe's appearance at the study door, an arrival which once again made my egress virtually impossible.

'For God's sake, let Jenny through to go and get Vine!'

Lady Lovescombe snapped at her husband. 'It's too disgusting in here, Richard. I told you to lock the spirits up in the cellar.'

Before the naming of a place exciting to both Victor Crane and J. D. Hare could rouse the men to another, possibly more dangerous bout, I found myself pushed past Lord Lovescombe and down the stairs to the main hall. But Vine, satisfied the last guest had been admitted – or conceivably in search of Bluey Stavrakis and Johnny Bouzouki in an attempt to eject them from the premises – was nowhere to be seen.

'Walter Neet.' A face resembling a grub, ridged but also giving off a distinct impression of a slimy coating, looked up at me from above a gaily coloured cravat. 'We met that summer at Lovegrove. You've come down to witness the exhibition, I suppose?'

Only the tone of ill-concealed pique alerted me to the fact that the water-colourist, as obscure three years later as he had always been ('never heard of him' had been the verdict of Aunt Babs, herself a keen follower of the art scene and ex-pupil of the Camden School), was referring to an exhibition of pictures, perhaps mounted by Lord Lovescombe from his collection, and not to an *exhibition*, pronounced in an overdone Gallic accent, to which the Brigadier sometimes referred when talking of his trips to Montmartre as a bachelor before the war. That Bernard Ehrlich, whose fame had, on the other hand, increased in the past three years, his reputation showing no sign of remaining static like Neet's, would almost certainly be among those on show, would be particularly galling to the elderly artist. Ehrlich's representations of Carmen – among many others, including Lady Lovescombe herself and the heiress Nagra Pont – would infuriate Neet, whose sense of honour and decency had no doubt been much offended by the blown-up and distorted rendering of what Ethel, seeing a photograph of the picture in an arts magazine, had labelled 'Carmen's privates'. As well as this, Walter Neet had confided to me just before lunch at Lovegrove that he had fallen hopelessly and madly in love with Carmen, the inevitable romanticism which accompanies this state no doubt rendering him even more vulnerable to an attack of rage and envy. I replied that I hadn't known there was a show, that I had come in search of Vine – though some form of discretion warned me against explaining to the excitable painter (in any detail at least) the reasons for Vine's presence being urgently necessary. Neet, however, took the words out of my mouth.

'Crane been sick yet?' The tone was aggressive, and, as he edged nearer, I saw his grub-like complexion metamorphose, the transcendental hues of an Oriental moth replacing the uniform ridged and pitted sallowness. 'I think Anne Lovescombe should have her head examined.' Neet drew himself to his full height as if applying for the post of phrenologist to the Lovescombe household. 'I mean, Crane is a security risk,' he went on, raising his voice while perhaps meaning to lower it, so that Vine, who had suddenly appeared from the door to the dining-room, looked worriedly about him. 'There are members of the royal family here. Anthony Eden is here. Crane is a spy and a traitor and should be taken away immediately!'

Before there was time for this order to be carried out – assuming that Vine, in his role as bodyguard, was prepared to abandon the party and take Victor Crane off to some secure place – a burst of applause, similar to the excited clapping audible from the study, came from the dining-room. Neet's face, empurpled above and below a stripe of greenish-blue across the nose, came up closer to mine. 'Let's go in and have a look. Mind you, I think it's all the most absolute nonsense.'

These scenes of the summer before returned to me as Mick Scupper, agile though he might be in terms of social climbing, attempted unsuccessfully to circumvent the various abandoned cardboard boxes of Portobello market. If I was reminded by this of my 'blocked' exit from the study where Victor Crane disgraced himself in front of his brother-in-law and host, I was taken back even more forcibly to the night of Amy's ball by the presence on Aunt Babs' table of what now appeared to me as that symbol of lost innocence, the white china dove. And the final showman-like jump executed by Scupper as he cleared a consignment of rotting cabbages brought to mind, though not, it must be said, pleasurably, the occasion that evening in the dining-room of the Lovescombes' Regent's Park house when Amy was persuaded again and again, after Scupper had leapt in ahead of her, to come like a performing dog into the room from the side door; and, in front of an admiring audience, point to the portraits on the walls and say, 'And these are the Vandykes.' Yet it was only as Scupper made the last lap away from the vegetables and towards us into the junk market that I realized that it had been references to Victor Crane on the part of Ethel which were probably responsible for my return to the ballroom and memories of Amy's humiliation.

'I remembered what the book was – the scandalous novel I was talking about earlier.' Ethel, ignorant of the identity of Scupper and unable, presumably, to recognize him from those smudged photographs supplied by the *Daily Express* as he arrived at or left nightspots and débutante cocktail parties, talked on happily as I, only too aware of who he was, stared first at Scupper and then at the dove, spotted by him already on Aunt Babs' stall and as surely marked down by him as if reared for the shoot at the Lovescombes' northern seat, Castle Azeby.

'Victor Crane wrote a book about a brothel in Jacksonville, Florida,' Ethel said. 'Funnily enough, that dealer from Kent who supplies me with the Ballantyne books told me only the other day.'

If it was some time before anyone could put Ethel right, it took Scupper no time to see her puzzling over this misinformation and to pick up the Chelsea dove, which he did with a tenderness I found – although I would be hard put to explain why to my aunt later – particularly offensive. Possibly it was because the hurried near-rape I had witnessed on the upper floors of the Lovescombes' London house had been as far as might conceivably be imagined from the soft caress accorded to this potential (inanimate) possession; perhaps again I suffered vicariously for Amy, and now for the dove, as recipient of any attentions from Mick Scupper whatever.

'So what are you asking for this today, my dear Babs?' Scupper said. I was sickened to see that some kind of relationship, no doubt since the sale of the Watts, had also been struck up between my aunt and Scupper. It gave me, therefore, a slight, sharp sense of relief when the art auctioneer now noticed me and registered dismay.

'Jenny!' Scupper's teeth, suddenly reminiscent of Red Riding Hood's grandma's, gleamed against a background of tomatoes and a tower of the newly imported and exotic sweet pimento. 'Long time no see. It was Amy's ball, wasn't it?' And, as if registering my expression of disbelief at his brazening out what had after all been an occasion of maximum embarrassment, including the offer on Lord Lovescombe's part of a horsewhipping (none of this resulting, as by now was patently clear to the rest of the world, in a shot-gun or any other type of wedding), he added quickly, 'Coming to the bash up north, I suppose? Care for a lift?'

It was impossible to ascertain whether Scupper was, so to say, proffering 'hush money' on the seduction scene in the shape of a lift all the way to Castle Azeby (I remembered the strong desire on the part of both Amy and Candida to ride in Scupper's Thunderbird in our last term at St Peter's together, and the rumour that such a car, a new and exciting arrival from the States, had been seen waiting at the corner of Brook Green to bear Carmen away instead) or whether the discovery of the Chelsea dove, as recognizable to him as it was to myself, was the blackmailing reason for the suggestion. Aware of my new-found position of power, I turned down the lift, this time with a touch of Candida's prim righteousness in my voice. Briefly excited by this – or so I had to suppose – Scupper seized my elbow and directed his not inconsiderable charm down at me, his quiff of hair dancing over his brow in the mild September breeze. 'Come on, Jenny. You may find it impossibly vulgar, but this time it's a pink Cadillac. Most girls rather like it, actually.'

The drawl, admired as much at the time by my school companions as the quiff, must have annoyed my Aunt Babs, for I saw that she suddenly took back the white dove from Scupper and covered it with an Indian shawl – mothball-smelling and badly in need of repair, for sale at two shillings and sixpence – as if (or so my over-stimulated imagination had to suggest) it were a baby, unwanted, possibly illegitimate (as in those days all children were stigmatized who were not born within conventional wedlock, the hippy lovechild being a long way in the future) or, also possibly, the baby of a wicked seducer such as Mick Scupper and an innocent girl.

Scupper must have seen some of these thoughts flash through my mind, for he withdrew his hand hastily from my arm and pulled the shawl away from the white dove. 'It looks like one of those fake Chelsea doves of the 1870s,' Scupper said. 'How about five pounds?'

'He must be joking!' The arrival of Roly Marr, the bright young dealer from under the bridge, was unusually welcome. Tired though I was of hearing Roly's descriptions of evenings with the 'old queens' of the antique world (suggesting first to me, in my ignorance, Helen of Troy and Cleopatra at the very least) and their dinner parties, frequently, it seemed, in the windows of their own shops, where 'toast was thrown in a silver bowl' and consumed in front of whoever might be passing, I felt that only Roly Marr at this stage would be able to dissuade Aunt Babs from parting with the dove at the very time when I was about to rescue and return it to its grateful owner.

'That's the real thing.' Roly Marr directed ice-sharp eyes in the direction of Scupper, whom he, unlike Ethel, had instantly recognized; Scupper's equally pale eye-lashes batted a moment while he worked out a reply. 'And I can tell you what book you're thinking of,' Marr continued as Ethel stood staring at us all, a bundle of rain-soaked *Common Readers* under her arm. 'You're not thinking of Victor Crane at all. You're thinking of Stephen Crane. He wrote *The Red Badge of Courage*.'

Scupper, frowning at the change of subject, suddenly took his chance and lifted the dove unceremoniously from its Indian resting-place. 'It is rather fine,' he said in a tone deliberately vague, even faintly insulting, as if the bird had, like an ill-trained pet, narrowly avoided soiling him. 'Perhaps a tenner, Babs, wouldn't you say?'

'Certainly not!' My aunt, alerted by Roly Marr, had clearly seen the unpalatable alternatives of trouble with 'bent gear' or the folly of giving it away for a song. 'It's not for sale.'

'Well, well!' Roly grinned at me and then at Ethel, as if to make sure that we were included in the drama. 'In that case, dear, you'd better give it back to the young lady. And . . .' – he turned to Ethel with the cheeky insouciance of the powerful jester, enjoying his temporary ability to set the scene – 'it was Stephen Crane's wife who ran the brothel in Jacksonville, Florida. *The Red Badge of Courage* is certainly not a scandalous novel, I can assure you.'

'Fancy that!' remarked poor Ethel, as an exercise book, the contents running inkily from the nervous spillage of the remains of a cup of tea in her other hand, tumbled to the pavement. 'I wonder if this is worth anything,' she added wildly, as her and Roly Marr's heads bumped in retrieving it. 'There was a bookish sort of young man here yesterday who said he might buy it. He works for a publisher.'

Mick Scupper, evidently unable to bear any more delay in his purchase of the dove, held it aloft, the severity of his features and startling blond hair giving him the look of a Greek god, as worshipped by Classics masters at prep schools. 'Who did you say sold this to you?'

The question being addressed to Aunt Babs, there was an inevitable wait before any kind of answer was forthcoming. Even the wait, I saw with an increased feeling of apprehension, would hardly benefit anyone, as the head of Carmen now became clearly visible on the far pavement behind the banana and coconut stall. She appeared to be looking into the window of an ironmongery store, where kettles and household cleaning apparatus, neither immediately associable with Carmen's *train de vie*, were set out on display.

'Carmen Bye,' Roly Marr said quickly, having spotted her too. 'She brought it in this morning, didn't she, Babs? I told Babs to have nothing to do with it,' he went on loudly as my poor aunt, apparently caught out in a dishonest act, made several vain attempts to explain the conditions of her purchase, these being assurances from the 'young lady' that she had been given the dove as a birthday present by an uncle and had nowhere to put it, as she was acting in a touring company and frequently on the road.

'Carmen!' said Mick Scupper, in a tone difficult to fathom, but seeming to contain, as it veered from surprise to acceptance, a wily ruse along the way. 'Well, that's all for the best,' he went on enigmatically.

'My God!' Roly Marr, determined not to be outshone

in this play of discoveries and retributions, snatched the exercise book – not so unlike, I reflected, the 'rough' books which Amy, instead of maths and algebraic formulae, had filled with representations of Scupper – and waved it as high as the dove, which was still held high by Scupper and must have been visible to Carmen as she turned away from the vacuum cleaners and dustbins on offer in the store. 'You don't realize!' Marr's voice, high and slightly contrived at the best of times, now degenerated to a squeak. 'This exercise book belonged to Virginia Woolf! Good heavens, Ethel, who did you say had shown interest in it yesterday?'

'A young man who said he was a publisher in Bedford Square. He asked me who Virginia Woolf was,' Ethel said in a slow, painstaking tone as Carmen, turning and seeing the dove and Mick Scupper joined, or so it must have looked to her, in some holy and unbreakable alliance, scrambled over the packing cases and advanced towards us. 'It did come with a job lot of the *Common Reader*,' Ethel added, as if this information could in some way solve all the mysteries of the valuable and anonymous objects deposited on her and my aunt's stalls in the course of a morning. 'What does it say?' She peered at the smudged writing as if the entire contents of the book would yield themselves up to Roly in much the same way as a picture, painted over, 'school of', forged or genuine, gives up the secrets of its provenance to the connoisseur.

Unexpectedly, Roly Marr dashed the copy book on to an adjacent pile of turnip tops. 'I hate Bloomsbury,' he muttered. 'Why don't you decide what you're going to sell, Ethel my darling, instead of letting people dump rubbish like this on you?'

Before there was time for Ethel – or any of us, for that matter – to register Roly Marr's taste in literature, the almost simultaneous sounds of china smashing and Carmen screaming, followed by loud imprecations from Mick Scupper, brought a temporary excitement to the market, several of the old clothes stallholders coming down from their coverts of moth-eaten furs and dead men's suits to pursue the disaster. Before I had time, too, to reflect that this was probably the only satisfactory ending for the dove (other possibilities, such as returning it to the 'House in the Woods' or – which had crossed my mind but which I dismissed as over-sentimental – Scupper 'buying' it for nothing from Aunt Babs and giving it as a wedding present to Amy and Crispin being equally unsatisfactory), the sound of a slap on a face made me turn quickly from my defensive position behind Ethel's books and, like the rest of the crowd, actually begin to digest the proceedings.

Carmen's fierce beauty at first drew sympathy from pretty well all the onlookers. It was clear that she had been insulted, possibly physically abused, by Scupper, whose Germanic good looks brought him little admiration from those whose experiences in the war had been uncomfortable to say the least, the option of evacuation or foreign exile being in the main denied to them. Carmen's slap, at that particular time, was, unfairly, extremely popular; and as it was hardly the moment to explain to the crowd that their heroine had stolen the bird in the first place, I decided to make a getaway as quietly and quickly as possible. Aunt Babs' distress I would cope with later, when the whole story of Carmen's theft at Lovegrove would be added to my aunt's list of reasons why no one should go to stay with 'people like that', as if the lax morals and abundance of servants enjoyed by the Lovescombes were in some way conducive to criminal behaviour on the part of the guests. I might even be persuaded to desist from going to the wedding at Castle Azeby, whether wafted there in a pink Cadillac (as I had seen Aunt Babs' fear that I might be, the refusal of the lift being perhaps only a feint, to be corrected later in private with Scupper) or in the third-class carriage with other friends of Amy's too indigent to travel in a more comfortable style.

This was a moot point, I knew, as an audience awaited further news of the family and its entourage, in particular Jasmine Tremlett, whose brazen conduct with every male mentioned had whetted the appetites of both Aunt Babs and Ethel, while the Brigadier, expressing disapproval, was always the first to ask me of her most recent exploits. I had told my aunt of the time, related to me by Amy, of Jasmine Tremlett's disappearance behind the cascade of water known as the Mare's Tail, near Castle Azeby, with Lord Lovescombe. This thirst for further information meant that my sidelong exit from the market scene not only did not go unremarked, but was accompanied, in my clumsy haste, by the wedding invitation knocking a pile of Ethel's books askew and restraining me for several painful minutes longer than I wanted.

'Look at that!' Carmen, anxious now to deflect attention from the marks of her stinging slap on the face of the stunned and immobile Scupper, pointed gleefully at the obtruding oblong of card, which, rather than allow it to be trampled in the vegetable refuse, I had by now pulled out of my pocket altogether. I was embarrassedly aware that the legend on the card was probably of a great deal more interest to many members of the crowd than *The Red Badge of Courage* or, to say the least, the notebook of Virginia Woolf.

'So you've been asked to Amy's wedding!' Carmen was by now addressing me in front of a faithful group of listeners, some of the old-clothes sellers having drifted back to their stalls after Aunt Babs' grim brushing away of the shattered fragments of the dove. 'I wouldn't dream of going. I'll be in Portugal, actually.'

'Carmen!' Scupper had found his voice, if not his composure. Wary of taking Carmen's arm in the nonchalant manner with which he had taken mine, he nevertheless edged towards her, the hard core of the audience backing nervously away from a possible continuation of the fight. 'We ought to go and sit somewhere and have a good chat,' Scupper said in a tone which he obviously considered to be 'reasonable' but which triggered torrents of laughter from Carmen. 'And Jenny . . .' – he turned to me as if my presence was suddenly seen to be essential to the settling of an old score – 'Jenny, you'll come with us to the pub, won't you?'

Looking back, I can only wonder that it didn't occur to me at the time to insist, as a mediator, on the British 'smoothing over' of differences between the two of them. Without the open war apparently declared on that day in a mush of rotting vegetables beside my aunt's stall, it seems likely enough that the impulse to terrorism, latent in Carmen from the start, might not have grown, to explode fifteen years later outside the bridal display window of Harrods. I might, I've come to think since, have changed, or at least modified, one portion of British history if I had sat down in a pub with Carmen and Scupper; for while there's no doubt that bombs would have been set off anyway at their appointed time in history, it's also true that Carmen, a 'wrong-doer' from her earliest years at St Peter's, greatly increased the danger to 'innocent people' (as Aunt Babs called civilians, this term to be much disputed by Leopold Tarn on the evening of his one, disastrous visit to my aunt's house, he announcing that 'innocence' amounted to little more than extreme right-wing views). I told Scupper, however, that I was doing something already and couldn't come; and Carmen's answer was also in the negative but a great deal more strongly couched.

'You stupid bastard! Why d'you think I'd sit down in a pub with you?' For all her bravado, it was clear that Carmen was upset – 'tears before bedtime', as I heard Ethel mutter as she ruffled the pages of the despised and now mud-stained Woolf notebook. Possibly the breakage of the dove, long hoarded by Carmen against a rainy day or held on to perhaps as some sort of sentimental memento of friendship with Amy and the visit to Lovegrove (despite the very unwelcome ending to the day), had distressed her more than she would care to admit. Scupper, as I now saw – for it was too late to try and bring any kind of harmony between them – was only too ready to use Carmen's refusal of his offer of a drink to declare hostility, his tone being one (or so he must have considered) of the enraged liberal: the stentorian end-result, however, coming out far louder than anything I had heard emanating even from the Brigadier on the occasion of a toe-stubbing – frequent in Aunt Babs' knick-knack-littered sitting-room.

'It is I who would run a risk by sitting down with you,' bellowed Scupper. 'With a thief, I may say! You realize, Miss – whoever you are – that that exquisite representative of the Chelsea school, *circa* 1760, was the property of your friend Amy's "Uncle Si"?'

That Carmen was now cast as a friend of Amy was mildly surprising, especially as Scupper's own claims to intimacy with Amy were a great deal more easy to prove, a bonding, indeed, of which I had been the reluctant witness. Carmen, apparently as uninvited to the wedding as she had been to the ball, could turn and attack Scupper on this issue; and this she proceeded to do.

'They wouldn't ask you up if they knew Amy had a bun in the oven!' Carmen's face was dark with rage. Aunt Babs and Ethel, shocked both by the indiscretion and the information – though probably more by the former, Aunt Babs having learnt from her Italian– German cousins, relics of a Jamesian world of cosmopolitan art and manners, that it was wrong to 'trail your coat in the piazza' – looked pointedly at the backs of a now hastily dispersing crowd. 'And you know perfectly well who I am,' Carmen bellowed. 'As for you – babysnatcher! Jailbait-maker! Ugh!'

This last exclamation of disgust brought the unpleasant realization that the Thunderbird car parked at the corner of Brook Green and the road where St Peter's red brick blushed half-seen behind portcullis-like gates had in all probability been Scupper's, and that Carmen's boasts of being met there by a sheikh and taken to tea at the Ritz were probably also correct, the only inaccuracy being that the sheikh was Scupper, using his shark-shaped vehicle complete with American police siren, to lure Carmen away long before the embarrassing episode of both Amy and Candida falling in love with him and needing no luring at all. My aunt, thinking, as I sensed, of the proffered lift to Castle Azeby in the pink Cadillac, shot me an agonized look, while Roly Marr, silent until now in contemplation of the Castle Azeby wedding invitation, looked up and announced that he had heard that Rubens and Teniers were very well represented at Castle Azeby. 'I might even pop up,' Marr mused, surprising me again by the feeling of general proprietorship inspired by the Lovescombe family in the most unlikely quarters. 'I've been meaning to go and have a look for ages. This'll spur me on. I'll stay with the Cleggs. I gather they've got a house party for it. The Tremletts are staying with them. Barbaric but better than nothing.'

Roly Marr's social planning, whether it was intended or not, had the effect of ending the bitter exchange between Carmen and Scupper – not that Scupper had had a chance of getting much of a word in. Left with his ripostes buried inside him, he instead looked angrily at Roly Marr and strode away from the scene, ungathered shards of the white dove crunching under heel; and I had to admit that for a moment I felt sorry for him, though this sensation was soon superseded by the memory of Scupper's rapacious and thoroughly undesirable ways, ways which, according to Carmen and her 'sisters' in a later incarnation, were the ways of all white male imperialist chauvinist pigs.   Carmen must have seen something of my ambivalent reactions to this scene, for she took my arm and said we should go to Chelsea together, to her friend's house, and have a coffee; and all this under the worried gaze of Aunt Babs, who, aware that my attempt to obtain linen napkins in Sloane Square had been fruitless, was trying to persuade me to go to Harrods next, the day of the money-raising dinner looming all the time nearer and causing mild panic in our circle, especially for some reason the Brigadier.

'Don't worry about Harrods,' Carmen said in a tone meant to be reassuring to my aunt. 'We've all got to go there to buy something on Amy's list, haven't we, Jenny?' And she added in a loud aside, some of her previous audience having returned at the disappearance of Scupper, 'Can you imagine rich people like the Lovescombes making their friends buy them toast-racks and things like that? I've been up to Castle Azeby, you know, and they've got rooms full of toast-racks!' We were all silent as we envisaged this impossible trove. 'And they've got ninety indoor servants!'

Even for my Aunt Babs, this was going too far. The 'servant problem' of the thirties had been eradicated, in her mind, by the war and replaced by machines. Only Ethel, who showed little sign of having passed that era in her reading matter, seemed unshaken by this and nodded sagely, a whole Trollopian world clearly existing for her as imperishably as before. 'But they still say there isn't room for Jasmine Tremlett,' Carmen added, hoping this time perhaps to attract the attention of Roly Marr. 'Even with forty bedrooms and all those trained domestics.' Carmen licked her lips at the munificence of Castle Azeby, while I, realizing that Lovegrove would seem a modest and easily manageable house in comparison with the northern estate, felt suddenly too inadequate to go up there to the wedding at all. 'It's because she's Lord Lovescombe's mistress, that's why!'

Before Roly Marr could protest (which he was clearly on the point of doing: I was to discover later that Marr used Jasmine Tremlett much as a gamekeeper uses a decoy, persuading her with gifts and 'discounts' to bring her wealthy lovers to his flat in Eaton Terrace, where he kept his more valuable wares) Carmen obviously decided that enough was enough and practically pushed me down the pavement and away from the market. 'You must meet Nagra, Jenny,' she said as we walked along. And, while we were still calculatedly within earshot of my aunt and Ethel, 'You must try a reefer with Nagra and me and Jules tonight. Jules has a house in the Atlas mountains, you know, and he's got the most heavenly consignment of kif, from Tangier.'

CHAPTER THREE

It was hard to know, from the vantage point of Harrods' Bridal Department just a few weeks after this scene, which was the most disturbing information of the day, Amy's rumoured pregnancy vying with the breakage of the Lovescombe family heirloom for first place, while the proffering by Carmen of drugs would certainly be alarming to my Aunt Babs.

Like shadows of a future so alien to the way of life in those days that the most adventurous of science-fiction writers (a race which at that time was keen to concentrate on visitations from outer space) would have been unable to predict it, the 'inner space' dictated by hallucinogens, like the space to be commandeered by advertising and the new vistas of gratuitous violence, was all visible that year, for whoever had the eyes to see it; and if a chill of premonition – one of many I suffered that year – descended on me as I stood among the white ribbons in the Bridal Department that day, it was as much due to the presence of Carmen as anything else. Carmen encapsulated (to my aunt, at least) the extremes of vulgarity, from 'drawing attention to oneself' to third-degree murder, as the theft and demolition of the Lovegrove dove now very likely appeared to my aunt. The gift for self-advancement and the desire for an audience manifest in Carmen's indiscreet oratory were matched, of course, by Scupper's behaviour at Amy's ball the summer before; but for all my relating of the tale to Aunt Babs and Ethel, they had seen nothing strange in Scupper's use of a débutante for his own promotional purposes (Roly Marr had only shortly before announced details of the impending sale at Christie's of the Lovescombe Vandykes 'for family reasons'). Both women were so imbued, presumably, with the idea that a director of a famous art auctioneers, as Scupper then was, must be the epitome of respectability that his evident corruption and unpleasantness went quite unnoticed by them.

To see Nagra Pont, too, was to remember the scene of the broken dove, for 'I'm staying at Nagra's tonight,' Carmen said, as we left the refuse of the market and made our way to Westbourne Grove, the rejected Scupper glaring after us after returning and trying to buy a set of Kipling from Ethel at a knockdown price on the grounds that several of the volumes were 'foxed'; 'and she can give you a lift up to Castle Azeby in the family Bentley, you know. She's absolutely rolling!'

I had somehow registered the 'rollingness' of Nagra Pont from her brief appearance at Lovegrove at the time of our ill-fated summer visit. Nagra was one of the pale mistresses of the painter Bernard Ehrlich (Carmen being the dark and Bacchic type the famous artist sometimes seemed to prefer), and I'd heard she was an heiress to some great steel fortune.

'No,' Carmen was saying as we got off the bus at the

World's End and came down on the King's Road, still in that era the demesne of small greengrocers, elderly eccentrics and the odd rich couple, 'it was Nagra who told me the news about Amy. Isn't Scupper a bastard? That's why I hit him, actually,' Carmen went on in a tone liable to various interpretations, the first being that she was making this up as she went along. 'Poor Lady Lovescombe, she'd be so upset if she knew,' Carmen added equally unconvincingly. We walked up Chelsea Manor Street and turned into a red-brick conglomeration by the name of Rossetti Gardens Mansions. Carmen paused, and stood to face me a moment, her turbulent dark mane and huge, suddenly soulful eyes bringing to mind those paintings of Lizzie Siddal as painted by William Morris (indeed, as I well knew from Ethel's enthusiasm for the school, Burne-Jones, Rossetti and Morris had all lived here in Chelsea, on the river with a menagerie of peacocks and an elephant for company). I thought instinctively of the contrast between Carmen as the great Utopian would have painted her and her actual portrait by Bernard Ehrlich, where a hirsuteness not normally represented by the Pre-Raphaelites was unmistakably the dominant feature.

'Doesn't Amy want to marry Crispin Hare, then?' I asked Carmen.

'You must be joking!' Carmen shot me a quick glance of contempt. 'The Lovescombes want her to, that's all.' Scanning a panel of names, Carmen suddenly muttered 'Pont!' and pressed a bell. A window high above us opened almost at once. Nagra Pont looked out, and her fair hair hung down over us like the silken rope so useful to Rapunzel – reminding me once again of Amy, whom I had seen, in the love-crazed language of Candida Tarn, as imprisoned at the top of her parents' London house in much the same way – until it was time for her to come 'down' and 'out', that is.

'What about Mick Scupper?' I realized too late that my interest in Amy had precluded me from asking what Carmen had been doing with the Chelsea dove all those years, and why she had, so fatally, decided to sell it to my Aunt Babs that morning. Nagra Pont had thrown a bunch of keys to the pavement; and her hair, now vanishing back in through the window, made a brief gleam of gold before disappearing altogether. Carmen gazed affectionately up at the disappearing pony-tail – a style that was then a recent import from the United States – and gathered up the keys. 'What *about* Scupper?' she said. 'By the way, Jenny, I'm going up to Castle Azeby with Nagra, so we can all go together.'

We entered a dark hallway, smelling more of slopped-down lino than of the millions scented by Carmen. This unpropitious entrance was, however, soon dismissed by Nagra Pont herself, more chatty on this occasion, it appeared, than at the time of her silent, withdrawn visit with Ehrlich to Lovegrove. (It was to occur to me that if Carmen was a 'whore' in Ehrlich's painterly imagination, then Nagra Pont, with her pale eyes and hair, would stand for a *belle dame sans merci*. How Lady Lovescombe or Jasmine Tremlett, both subjects of the elusive artist, were seen, it would be hard to say, unless they simply represented bundles of meat and bone as depicted.)

'It's only a flat for a moment or two,' Nagra Pont announced mystifyingly, as she rounded the lino-clad staircase to greet us, Carmen tossing back her keys as she did so. 'Our real house is round the corner in Cheyne Walk.'

It was difficult to make out what the Pont family idea of reality or its opposite was likely to be, though Carmen soon explained (when Nagra, once we were in the flat, went off to get glasses and drinks) that a place as 'ordinary' as this flat (despite its large rooms and leafy outlook, giving the place an air of solid but artistic respectability that would have been found most desirable by my Aunt Babs and Ethel) did not in some important way exist as far as Nagra and her relatives were concerned; whilst extravagant and eccentric follies, even if virtually uninhabitable, were as 'real' as could be desired.

Once we'd got into the drawing-room and our eyes were acclimatized to the light, or the lack of it, I was more taken up with actually being able to see Nagra's other guests than with thoughts of the possible insubstantiality of Rossetti Gardens itself. A heavy-set man lay sprawled across a *chaise longue*, which, embroidered with tattered, dragon-emblazoned silk, seemed to boast of past days in surroundings both more real and more fantastic. That he was asleep was only discernible when Carmen addressed him in her usual sergeant-major's tones.

'Hello, Jules. Wake up, for God's sake!'

The man stirred; a small rustling from a cushioned corner of the room showed the presence of what seemed to be a nest of girls as pale as Nagra, and thus probably sisters or cousins; and Nagra herself returned from the kitchen, holding two unwashed glasses and a bottle of bourbon whisky.

'Shall we have an old-fashioned?' She looked round at

the room overshadowed by the trees and thick greenery outside, and I was reminded again of a painting by Burne-Jones, where a group of maidens, bowed down by the weight of their tresses, seem about to fall into a deep sleep – in this case probably following the lead of the exhausted knight, fresh off his steed at Camelot, who has brought them, at long last, the forbidden stuff of dreams.

'Jenny! Have one!' Nagra Pont said, as the man woke for just long enough to pull a paper packet from under the chair. 'Go on, Carmen! And no more for the little ones!'

The rest of that evening, taking place so short a time before the date set for Amy's wedding, was to remain a blur for me, the explanations I demanded at the time from Carmen on the subject of the possible 'triangle' between Scupper, Candida and Amy either going unanswered or, as was quite likely the case, receiving long and elaborate answers which the 'reefers' so freely distributed by the half-sleeping Jules obliterated almost instantly. I remember a young man with a beard – this unusual enough in those days – giving a further impression of medievalism when he appeared in the flat; there was a skiffle record, too, and the reedy voice of the young man as he sang along with it, reiterating many times that he had on board 'all pig iron'. And I was to see the various poses of Nagra's guests as they came and went, some in breeches and some in long gowns, as the stance of the people in the pictures at the Lovescombes' London house, on the night of the ball: as if, perhaps, Carmen's tales of Amy and Scupper and Candida, while incomprehensible to me in the ordinary way, translated themselves into images of a distant court, itself adorned with allegorical and mythological scenes.

As I dreamed, Scupper and the portraits on display at the Lovescombe house in Regent's Park merged together, as did Amy and her Titian-haired cousin Henry Azeby, to make a tapestry mystifying and mercenary. It was apparent that Amy's little masque, as Scupper fondly called it, had been put on for the benefit of possible buyers of the Vandykes, no doubt going on sale to afford further space for Lord Lovescombe's collection of modern art (or so I thought naïvely, unaware of the extent of Lord Lovescombe's gambling habits or, for that matter, of the number of other ménages he was likely to be supporting – as it emerged many years later – for it was not only Jasmine Tremlett who was the beneficiary, in her lifetime, of an income and a flat in St John's Wood, this as far removed as was then possible from her husband Jim Tremlett's seedy premises of *Margin* in Greek Street).

'And these are the Vandykes!' Scupper's voice rang in my head as Jules, rolling more joints, held them out sleepily to us. And as Nagra's strangely garbed friends strolled the room the portraits on the walls of the Lovescombes' dining-room stared down at me in my dream of past and present at the ball: 'Roll up! Roll up! Ladies and Gentle *Men*!'

It had been Henry Azeby who came up to me as I ran from the wrath of Lady Lovescombe, and, with a leer that was particularly offensive, said that 'Mick and Amy' were 'doing it' on the top floor.

It wasn't hard to suspect Scupper of seducing Amy with the intention of securing her money. Scupper had finally realized, perhaps, his mistake in preferring Candida to Amy at the time of our abortive visit to Lovegrove. But, whatever the reason for his behaviour, I had no desire to be seen either by him or Amy on the upper landing on the night of her ball. It was due to my need to escape Victor Crane and J. D. Hare that I had wandered into a part of the house I had never been to before. And it was entirely my bad luck that the handle of the first door I tried let me half into an unmistakable scene of débutante seduction: net ball-dress rumpled in a bustle of sheets and two figures prone on a child's eiderdown. I closed the door hastily and walked on. A sharp woody smell – I thought of Lovegrove again, but I couldn't be sure why – emanated from the half-open door of one of the other rooms on the landing where Amy, according to Candida, had been incarcerated as a young adult. Entirely from desperation, I pushed open the door and went in.

Ludo was standing at the far end of the room between two tall windows looking out on high chimneystacks. A grey sky edged with dark red glowed above the reaches of Camden Town and Regent's Park, where a blackness, fed by trees, took over; and in his pose, one foot resting on a chair, head low as he appeared to stroke some object, shoulders narrow with concentration, I thought with a sudden pang of my midnight visit to the unknown regions of Lovegrove, the dark passages and rooms which, after a twisting and turning and a falling in that almost forgotten part of the house, had led to an old schoolroom, a sofa rumpled from generations of inattentive children, and Ludo caressing a head of pale hair, which later turned out to be the (only visible) part of Amy.

This time, Ludo's stroking movements could be seen to be directed towards a gun. The wooden handle was, in fact, undergoing a polishing; and the smell of resin and polish must have returned me to the gun-room at Lovegrove, a place described by Amy and only briefly glimpsed by me; a place which, for obvious reasons of safety, was visited by Lord Lovescombe or his son, while Victor Crane or Walter Neet, say, were less likely to gain admittance. Ludo glanced up, and held out the gun so that the inscribed silver mount, still tarnished, caught a dull gleam from the overhead light. He looked at me with his half-rueful look (or so I, an incorrigible women's magazine reader, described to myself those glances, half Amy's, half his own, which had haunted me all the years since I had first known him) and made to hand me the weapon, so that I had to walk up to him and take it by the butt.

'Well, Jenny!' Ludo's voice had that same self-deprecating, slightly mournful note that I remembered from the summer visit to Lovegrove – a note, as I came to think, which was deemed expedient in those days for a young man shouldering the responsibility of his future inheritance: 'I am nothing,' it seemed to say; 'I can do nothing, the place and possessions are everything.'

'You've been in Nigeria?' I was painfully conscious of sounding like Ethel's rendering (after a few drinks) of *Private Lives*. 'Was it – fun, there?'

'There was a grapefruit tree outside my house,' Ludo said. He laughed. 'So I could pick one every morning for breakfast. Look, Jenny –' I started back with the gun as his hand fastened on my arm. 'You know how to polish

66

silver, don't you? Spit on it and then rub with this. Your spit may be better than mine, you know.'

I admit I didn't know what to make of Ludo's almost feverishly flirtatious manner. It passed through my mind that Ludo too knew of the goings-on in the bedroom down the passage; that the nursery floor, designated, for all I knew, for the romps of brother and sister since early childhood was considered by him to be particularly his territory; and that Scupper's violation of it had driven him temporarily mad. Yet – which I had no pleasure later that night in admitting to myself – a part of me thought also that in Ludo's years as an ADC in Nigeria he had nursed fond thoughts for me, the isolation of his position and consequent lack of 'suitable' female company increasing the possibility (and here I escalated at speed in my foolish estimation of the situation) of real love.

'I tell you what,' Ludo said, taking the gun (which, it must be said, was not noticeably improved by the spit and polish just administered); 'let's leave here and go out in the park. Like a walk, Jenny? I'll show you a secret garden no one knows about except me – us,' he added suddenly, as if it were too painful to exclude his sister, even at such a moment of betrayal, from his speech or memory. 'It's not really part of the park as such. It's called the Blue Garden and it belongs to the college down the road. All the flowers there are blue. We can climb in through a gap in the railing. Come on!'

In Ludo's voice, as well as concealed despair, there was a good deal of genuine affection; and I had the feeling, fleeting though it turned out to be, that we were indeed like some married couple, long separated by the vicissitudes of life and career and now, finally, reunited; though how Ludo managed to convey this I don't know. The atmosphere he gave out, I suppose, was so different from the chill of exclusion which had been following me around all evening. That the 'Blue Garden' had clearly been a trysting place for brother and sister made it only, in that moment of folly and trustingness, more special to me; for hadn't I loved Amy first? And the knowledge, to come to me in the bitter dawn, that I was of all my contemporaries the most sealed still in adolescent fantasy (both Carmen, with her brutal view of the world, and Candida, with her higher education, representing the acme of maturity in comparison with myself: even Amy, at least, preparing herself for a life as a wife and, presumably, mother), was of no consolation whatsoever. I knew, too, that I could expect little sympathy from Aunt Babs: would not dare even to confide my feelings for a scion of a family so mistrusted and disapproved of by her; while to find oneself a lifelong Cinderella who was for one night the consort of a prince would bring a good deal of amusement from Ethel, purveyor as she was of second-hand editions of Andrew Lang's *The Red*, *Yellow* and *Green Fairy Book*. The fantasy might have broken sooner if the sudden eruption into the room of Victor Crane had not apparently bound us closer together, there being nothing the young like so much as mocking a ridiculous person of middle age.

'Dear boy!' Crane peered round as if expecting to find a member of the Cabinet waiting to test his authentic accent. 'Seen Dickie anywhere?'

This was the first time, to my knowledge, that Richard Lovescombe, Amy's father, had been referred to as

'Dickie', and both Ludo and I burst out giggling, our laughter binding us together – or so I thought – in a perpetual Blue Garden, where the sayings of the outside world would be for ever unheard by us. Such were the expectations of 'romance' at that time – or that at least is how I tried later to excuse myself – the general atmosphere of undying love and unspoken promise being reinforced by the strains of 'There's a Small Hotel' wafting up to us from the band in the ballroom below.

'Your pa.' Victor Crane suddenly sat down on the floor, as if ordered by the lordly host just mentioned to lower himself as quickly as possible. 'Thing is, there's been a bit of a bust-up down there. Thought he'd better come and sort the whole thing out.'

Crane's Wodehousian tones, as I was to discover, were adopted by many of those who betrayed their country; and showed a marked schoolboyishness, while the use of funny voices and disguises emphasized a refusal to grow up. Certainly Crane's rather unaccomplished imitation of an irascible peer combined with minor public schoolmaster suggested that the 'bust-up' he described had in some way involved him; while the sitting position he had suddenly assumed seemed to indicate the recent receipt of a severe reprimand. Ludo burst out laughing again. 'What's going on down there, then, Victor? Prime Minister met Colonel Nasser in the loo?'

'It's not so far off!' Crane was spluttering now, though whether this was due to an unnaturally large intake of Lord Lovescombe's Château Palmer (as identified by Roly Marr the next day) or from fear of his own unmasking, it was hard to say.

'Well, maybe we'd better go down and have a look,'

Ludo said, assuming a tone of mature authority which again, I must admit, gave me a certain sense of being the consort of the ruler of a fiefdom, an arbitrator of punishment and reward. 'And then we've got a date, haven't we, Jenny? In the Blue Garden, no less!'

I must say here that my confused memories of that evening of Amy's ball, inspired and lulled as they were by the marijuana supplied at Nagra Pont's flat, do at this point merge and interweave, so that it's hard to admit how much of a dream my visit to the Blue Garden actually was. As I lay in Rossetti Gardens Mansions, and Mrs Bolt, the charlady (her name reminiscent of the governess at Lovegrove, Miss Bolton, coverer of Lady Lovescombe's unclothed form at the time of the nude bathing in the pool of the Children's Garden) vacuumed crossly in those parts of the flat not filled with sleeping, hallucinating figures, I seemed to see myself in the Blue Garden. We walked on lawns cut like figures of eight among beds of lupins, delphiniums, pansies and Canterbury bells, the blue, like the blue of precious stones, invisible at night, but there because Ludo said it was there; and as we walked Ludo told me he loved me, said we should get married one day. Not even at its most uncontrolled, however, did my memory allow this to happen, before the scene on the upper landing, though possibly exaggerated and distorted by the 'weed' (as Carmen, with a superior air, referred to it), was replayed for me.

The first person to round the top of the staircase on that fateful evening was Lord Lovescombe. As in a dream

– or as if I were already caught in the dream that was to illuminate suddenly a dark corner, obliterated at the time by shame and a fear of social misdemeanour – he headed for his daughter's room and stood with one hand on the doorknob. At the same time, he caught sight of me and stood frozen, hand still in place.

I must have seemed to Amy's father by then a harbinger of ill fortune. At his magnificent ball I must have appeared to be the consort of Victor Crane at his least *sortable* (a word culled from Aunt Babs' Italian–German – and part American – Jamesian – cousins, the Stringers, who, to my own considerable embarrassment spoke still in the ancient, elitist terms of an Almanach de Gotha past); and I must have appeared, too, to encourage drink and disorderliness on the part of the future father-in-law of the bride – who, with the grim inevitability of such dreams, now rose on the stairs behind Lord Lovescombe, smile fixed at an uncertain angle on his face. Lord Lovescombe, as if set off like a marionette in one of those haunted houses on a seaside pier by the sight of J. D. Hare, turned the handle of Amy's door with a sharp click.

I looked on in silent agony at the workings of fate – or coincidence – or whatever had brought the two men to the top of the house together. In J. D. Hare's case, at least, the question was soon answered. 'Someone told me there was a stash of Paddy up here.' The novelist, having with difficulty reached the landing, looked round belligerently and at first incredulously, the vision of Victor Crane slumped on the floor of yet another room clearly seeming more likely to be a product of 'DTs' (I was unsure at the time of what these were supposed to be, the Brigadier claiming that the circling of one's room by a green woodpecker was a certain sign) than an ascertainable fact. Crane, however, shifted uncomfortably at the first sighting of J. D. Hare and spoke, given the circumstances, with admirable clarity. 'This is no time for talking about Paddy. There's one hell of a bust-up going on down there. For God's sake, Jack! No point in staying in an ivory tower for ever!'

It was hard to know what to make of this and successive remarks as Lord Lovescombe had by now opened the door of Amy's night nursery, gone two paces into the room and come out again. It was at this point that his eyes looked straight into mine – unfairly, I thought, as if Amy's seduction were just another schooldays prank organized by myself and others – and, remembering my name all over again, said loudly and firmly: 'Good evening, Jenny! We meet again. Shall we take our good friends downstairs?'

That Victor Crane and J. D. Hare were the good friends in question there could be no doubt. What prevented me – for as I had rightly supposed, I was by now the assumed protector of the old Comrade, his wife having long ago decided to go home – from having to help shepherd them both down a dangerous staircase was the noise of the bust-up, or what remained of it, coming up.

The sight of one of Lord Lovescombe's most dearly acquired pieces of modern art rising in the shape of a splintered ruff about the neck of the water-colourist Walter Neet must at least have removed paternal comments on Lord Lovescombe's part of horsewhipping Amy's seducer. That the canvas, a painting of the Neo-

Romantic school then in vogue and depicting a sea-shore, timbers of a boat, a moon and a forked tree, all of which were brooded over by a Greek matelot in stripes and beret, was the work of Sidney Carston, R A, brother of our art mistress at St Peter's, only became clear as Neet in turn rounded the bend in the stair and arrived puffing on the landing. There had been talk, I knew, of 'a Carston' for the collection of contemporary art at Lovegrove; but that one had long been in London – in the bicycle room where Amy entertained her friends and where odd, unwanted visitors, usually relatives of the Lovescombes, were told to sit until they could be granted an audience – I hadn't known. At any rate I felt grateful for the arrival of Neet, to take the heat off a potentially explosive situation.

It appeared that Bernard Ehrlich and Carmen had been responsible for the scandalous treatment of the painting (Neet's head went virtually unsympathized with). A 'fracas', as the wretched painter thickly put it, had broken out on the topic of modern art; and while Neet had had the bravery to tell Ehrlich exactly what he thought of his 'butcher's shops', the brooding painter of women's carcases had not in turn deigned to mention Neet's own 'efforts' (as the Brigadier innocently but hurtfully referred to my Aunt Babs' oils and gouaches) but had instead spoken scornfully of the whole Neo-Romantic school and had smashed a John Minton against the dining-room table before going next door and ripping the Sidney Carston, R A, from the wall. A brief fight, to which Vine had fatally tried to put a stop, had broken out, both Victor Crane, temporarily under the illusion that he was at the Gargoyle Club, and 'Bluey' Stavrakis, who, it was said by Carmen later, had just accepted Lord Lovescombe's collection of modern art in its entirety in settlement of a 'bad debt', joining in; only Carmen, as she was to boast – I believe she even expected some kind of reward for her enterprise – putting an end to the whole affair, while incidentally preventing the decapitation of Walter Neet by Bernard Ehrlich, by forcing the picture down over his head and providing a protective shield.

'This is absolutely intolerable!' Lord Lovescombe said. He spoke with a solemnity which implied a considerable experience in boardroom speeches and after-dinner oratory. 'Take that thing off at once!'

'My dear Richard!' Neet peered along the landing; and, seeing only the back view of J. D. Hare with a bottle of whisky, Paddy, indeed, to judge by label and colour of contents, the painter tottered towards the door of the room occupied by Amy and Mick Scupper. 'Best thing is I take it off in here,' he said. 'Thank God it isn't a picture of mine, that's all I can say!'

The voicing of these sentiments appeared to come as the last straw for Lord Lovescombe. I was glad, almost, that the laughter – what Ethel would have termed a snicker – that succeeded it from somewhere down the stairwell was so evidently male: to be accused of giving vent to open mirth at the obvious discomfiture of my host would have been almost unbearable.

I turned to catch Ludo's eye – still confident, I admit, that we were two minds and hearts working as one, interrupted this time only by a scene of priceless buffoonery.

Ludo stood staring ahead. I wondered whether occasions of his father's anger, Jove-like, overpowering in their intensity, had petrified him since he was a child.

Lord Lovescombe – who seemed every minute to be about to turn into Humpty-Dumpty, his banker's rotundity and egg-dome head contorting his features so that they appeared to slip as if already running from the shell – clearly was in no way comic to Ludo. Neet's relief at the safe condition of his own pictures, to him probably the most significant acquisitions made by his host to the famous collection of modern art, combined with the Harlequinesque pose he had adopted at the door of Amy's room, was farcical to the point of danger – the danger, of course, coming from the presence of Lord Lovescombe, whose famous temper, after an unexpected view of Amy with Scupper, could be counted on. (The scene in progress in the nursery would, for obvious reasons, go unremarked by both Crane and J. D. Hare, while Neet himself was impeded from seeing anything below the level of his chin.)

'What on earth's going on up here?' Henry Azeby came up the stairs in an apparently innocent state of consternation. And, before any of the unsuitably placed persons to whom he had addressed his inquiry could reply: 'I've come to tell you, Uncle Richard, that the Foreign Secretary is leaving. And the Princess has asked for her car.'

Lord Lovescombe visibly shrank at this information. Comparisons with a nursery-rhyme figure faded, and it was possible to witness the reshaping of a fattish, stocky man, whose evening pumps stuck out gleaming at the end of now verifiably human legs. The rest of us, however, seemed to be rendered invisible by this messenger from the outside world. The mention of a more potent fantasy, that of political power and royal favour, made

Neet's presence on the landing unimportant – hand out-stretched in the direction of Amy's door though it might be. Crane and Hare, in a distant bas-relief behind Ludo, also fell into a state of immobility. Amy herself, disgraced and now obliterated from Lord Lovescombe's mind as he juggled with the logistics of his departing guests, was as silent from inside her room as before – leading me to wonder if she had now escaped, as Candida had once hoped she would, on a rope of her own hair from the upper windows of the Lovescombes' house. Lord Loves-combe now made a sudden bustling movement, which emphasized even more strongly the powerlessness of his captives on the nursery floor.

'The Princess has asked for her car!' he repeated.

'Thank you, Henry. I'll go down at once!'

Lord Lovescombe and his cousin disappeared from sight. I turned to Ludo, hoping for an unbending, a beginning to our walk in the Blue Garden, a life that would be free of everything and everyone but ourselves. Ludo, as if he could sense my need – and also, no doubt, to circumvent the horror of the nursery door revealing its secrets once more – grabbed Walter Neet's hand with the apologetic haste of a man who is about to throw a dog out of a room before going out. If I found myself reflecting briefly that it would do Ludo no harm at all to see his sister lying in her virginal four-poster with 'that knave Scupper' (in the words of the Brigadier, on hearing from Aunt Babs the rumours of the art auctioneer's seduc-tion wiles and their result as put about in the market by Carmen) I banished my thoughts as soon as they came, knowing that Ludo's suspicions confirmed would hardly generate a romantic evening in the Blue Garden. Neet, with an expression of profound gratitude, allowed himself to be led in his ruff of canvas and oil into the room where Ludo, only a short time before, had been polishing his guns – the water-colourist's gratitude, as I saw, emanating from the fact that the room was hung principally with Walter Neets.

'My dear boy! I wondered where the *œuvre* had finally landed up!' It was hard to tell whether the painter was pleased or angry: on the one hand, the Neets, small and unassuming as they were, were at least all together (and were all, as I could now see, of a northern castle, surrounded by moors, with a distant view of a long waterfall – in all probability the Mare's Tail, behind which, according to Amy, Lord Lovescombe had sheltered with Jasmine Tremlett). On the other hand, as it was also possible to see reflected in the violent struggles in Neet's face, the pustules under his skin seeming to shove up with particular gusto as if the broken canvas round his neck served as some kind of palette for these unappetizing blobs, the collection of Neets was clearly in no way attached to Lord Lovescombe's famous collection, having been banished to the children's quarters at the top of the house. As he stood hesitating between the thankfulness originally expressed and a bitter venom born of a lifetime of insignificance when compared with, say, Bernard Ehrlich, Keith Vaughan or Graham Sutherland – or, as far as the art of the water-colour was concerned, Paul Nash – a door at the far end of the corridor opened. Through it a slender figure made its way down the landing towards us. The now recumbent figures of J. D. Hare and Victor Crane, who appeared from their sleeping positions at the top of the stairs to have been cut down just as they tried to rejoin a world to which they had no automatic right of entry, were daintily stepped over. I felt Ludo stiffen at my side. And, as if he had half given up hope of ever seeing her again, as if, in the enchanted circle of the Lovescombes' ball, some wicked fairy had intentionally kept them apart all evening, Ludo stretched out his hand in a bemused, happy greeting.

'Candida,' he said. 'I thought you'd never come!'

It was at that point impossible to make out what had prevented Candida, either partnerless at the ball or forced into the equally reluctant arms of a 'suitable young man' provided by one of Lady Lovescombe's henchwomen, from coming up and joining Ludo, if this was what they really wanted. The thought, impossible to dismiss, crossed my mind that Ludo and Amy had wanted in some way to share their love-making, Amy with a vulgar showman and her brother with an over-eager young girl – myself – to make a public spectacle of themselves, as my aunt would undoubtedly have put it. But the idea itself was too vulgar – and too unlikely – to take root. Had Ludo, tired of waiting for a tryst with Candida, decided to try and make her jealous by asking me instead of her to a secret garden in the park at this hour of the night? Such women's magazine thinking, again, proved my downfall, for by now Candida had come right into Ludo's room and was making an inspection of the small, framed pictures on the wall. I was reminded suddenly of photographs of royalty, a certain refined way of holding out one hand (white-gloved to the elbow, a fashion still adhered to, presumably, by Mrs Tarn and by the older members of the Lovescombes' circle). Her slightest movements appeared to be invested with an unusual importance; though, in the sleeping presence of the drunks on the upper floor, the necessity for this was at first obscure.

'I was kept downstairs longer than I thought.' Candida's voice was as clipped, prim and self-satisfied as ever. Confirming my invisibility, she walked past me right up to Ludo, whose lapels she now pulled at playfully. Her voice, I noted as I stood there unseen, had a gushing and trilling quality which could have emanated from the famous waterfall at Castle Azeby, as depicted by Neet. 'I do think, Ludo darling, that we're absolutely right to demolish the west wing at Castle Azeby. I mean, it's all bogus anyway, but who wants to have additions to something that's already a glorious fake?'

CHAPTER
FOUR

In view of such past mistakes – for this, inevitably, was how I came to see the whole progression of my feelings for Ludo: as someone playing blind-man's buff, on removing the blindfold, will react on discovering there is no one there – in view, as I say, of the shame and embarrassment suffered on the night of Amy's ball and relived in the marijuana den instigated by Carmen and Nagra Pont in Rossetti Gardens Mansions only a few days before Amy's wedding, the appearance in Harrods' Bridal Department of Candida came, if not exactly as a surprise, then as a harbinger of worse things to come.

I felt this, I suppose, because the occasion of the Castle Azeby wedding, particularly since the ill-omened smashing of the white Chelsea dove by Carmen, had become a dark tunnel from which there appeared to be no conceivable escape. Ethel, while wanting me to go north and return with impossible tales of princedoms set in water cascades, staircases of pure superfluous rain from the misty surrounding hills (or so Walter Neet's small, flat-edged pictures had tried to suggest, showing the spirals and balustrades of artificial water by adding spittles of white along the side of lawns and otherwise conventional garden walls) had also understood my feelings and gone so far as to suggest that I should refuse the invitation to the wedding and stay in London and concentrate on my work instead. She'd seen, I believe, my propensity to give credit where none was due: to credit, in short, the improbable; and was keener than Aunt Babs to curtail what she, as an avid reader, could see as a fatal flaw in my make-up, this being the confusion of fiction with reality. Already I had 'fallen' for the Lovegrove myth and its attendant dangers and seductions: now, having made a full recovery and got myself a job gilding mirrors of those who saw themselves reflected as the fairest of them all (albeit slightly distressed by the vagaries of war and taxation), Ethel was undoubtedly concerned that I should not reimmerse myself in the Lovescombe atmosphere. Aunt Babs, on the other hand, was so certain that her own dismissive inquisitiveness was shared by me – that her mantle of gentle scorn and sharp interest would protect me from the possibility of becoming tarnished by the very mention of the Lovescombes – that she was only too happy to see me set off in the direction of King's Cross and thence to what the Brigadier barkingly referred to as 'border country'. She had no idea, of course, of the fantasies I had entertained of living in this northern stronghold myself one day: of 'running' it even, as mistress of the upstart's castle set down in the hills by Lord Lovescombe's grandfather; and would certainly have considered this particular fantasy both vulgar and snobbish, whether or not inspired by the representations of rugged hero and dewy-eyed impoverished heroine of the women's journals of the time. Aunt Babs would have despised me, had she known, and recognizing this had increased the strain, causing me to promise her almost hysterically to bring a full account of the wedding to the audience in Portobello market (the account, it went without saying, to be as humorous and full of ridicule as possible) while Ethel, a connoisseur of the 'faraway' look of one too easily able to lose themselves in their inventions, would astonish Aunt Babs by saying in a quiet voice that she 'couldn't see any reason why the trip up there was necessary at all'.

Stung by this, Aunt Babs retaliated that she was aware of other, more important things going on in the world than the marriage of the Lovescombes' only daughter Amy to her cousin Crispin Hare. There was the ghastly foreign policy of the government, the disaster of Anthony Eden. Even earthquakes and the occasional flood had been known to be brought into the argument at this point, Ethel shaking her head and smiling enigmatically (which was clearly maddening to Aunt Babs) as her sole way of refuting my aunt's contention. On the very day of my visit to Harrods – as my aunt was quick to point out – there was the launching into space of Sputnik – indeed, my trip was made to seem downright frivolous when compared with this brave new odyssey, but I had, as a reason for going to Harrods, not only the need to buy a wedding present for Amy – 'Freudianly postponed', as my aunt's cousin Wolfgang would undoubtedly have put it – but the errand, fast becoming urgent, of finding 'cloth napkins' for Aunt Babs' fund-raising dinner party, the trip to Peter Jones having proved abortive. And Ethel, defusing the state of indignation and exaltation which was liable to overcome Aunt Babs at moments of stating strongly held political views or interesting new information on the state of the world, would reiterate that as I no longer had close friendships within the family there was really no obligation for me to go.

That I was going all the same only pinpointed – or so Ethel evidently thought – a major weakness in my character, that of being unable to refrain, as she, in her trade as purveyor of pulp fiction, might be tempted to put it, from turning the page and reading on. The chapters so far in the saga of my relations with Amy and her folk had been painful, but, if the book were closed, I might be the poorer for it – a belief, I must admit, to which it was hard to adhere when confronted by the sight of Candida in the Bridal Department of Harrods. For all that Amy – remembered by me so forcibly as a 'figure in white' (a transformation from her rather boyish self at school) dancing at her ball in a net dress, or engulfed in a sea of white muslin bed-hanging and embroidered linen sheets at the time of her seduction on the upper floors of the Lovescombes' London house – was the one who was about to get married, it was Candida who appeared, as she made a stately tour of the department, to be marked out as a bride. Seeing her pause by the breakfast sets – small trays bearing rose-patterned cups and saucers, egg-cups and miniature milk jug (there being two of everything except the jug, so that a picture of wedded intimacy, of two pairs of hands reaching from the wide recesses of a nuptial couch to add a droplet of milk to the early morning tea, was conjured up) – I decided to make a getaway before she saw me and came over. Another effort, that of banishing from mind the scene of Candida and Ludo on the landing of the Lovescombes' London house and the knowledge that came with it of her easy dominance of him, would be necessary once I had made my way to the place where I could reasonably expect to find napkins. By failing to buy Amy a wedding present, I could also quite reasonably find an excuse for failing to go to the wedding at all; a conclusion made all the firmer by Carmen's sudden arrival at my elbow, a bridal veil somehow attached to her person, so that fishnet tights, with holes showing a skin of surprising whiteness underneath, were, like the 'gear' in one of the more unsavoury *fin de siècle* 'naughty' photographs collected and sold by Roly Marr at his stall under the bridge, entwined with this symbol of a virginal purity. Carmen breathed heavily into my face, exuding garlic – still at that time almost unknown on these shores and an inevitable sign that the breather had recently feasted at Louisa's Bistro in Ebury Street where the bulb, dug in lumps into stale bread, was an accompaniment to Louisa's rudeness and (to some) entertaining ribaldry. Frequent glances over her shoulder, while relieving me of a constant reception of the stink, also indicated an advanced state of paranoia. 'For God's sake, Jenny, get me out of here! Where are the stairs down, anyway? Filthy old man!'

It became clear that Carmen was referring to the father of the bridegroom, J. D. Hare, now searching clumsily among 'going away' outfits for his prey. A cerise wool dress, pinned closely to the flanks of a mannequin – as if to underline the absence of any sort of bump in the wearer's tummy at the time of the wedding ceremony – teetered wildly as, seeing Carmen at last, he made his way towards us.

My desire was as great as Carmen's when it came to

beating a hasty retreat from the place. I had seen, in the far corner by a discreet pile of luggage (whether intended for a rapid departure from a disastrous honeymoon was unclear) a door leading to stairs, and the wonderful prospect of freedom. To reach it, having to pass the desk with the list, and Nagra Pont, would be inescapable; but the route to be taken would at least avoid J. D. Hare and, most importantly, Candida. I pulled Carmen after me, aware of a mermaid train of netting and various small objects caught up in it, dragging after us: china boxes too small to contain anything of domestic worth; badly designed corkscrews (inevitable provokers of marital discord); linen hand-towels promising housewifely misery by virtue of their demand to be laundered and ironed daily – all washing somehow in Carmen's wake, as if, like a ship finally leaving harbour, she had gathered barnacles in abundance before the trip. Remembering the occasion of the 'lifted' dove at Amy's uncle's house in the woods at Lovegrove, I decided this time to say nothing – imagining, and rightly, as it turned out – that the oddness of Carmen's appearance combined with the scattered harvest in her train might be taken as a fashionable costume. (The new restaurant of the time, *La Popote*, had an example of this look which had recently brought a shudder to my aunt when taken there by the Brigadier. Netting draped across the ceiling of *La Popote* and studded here and there with a conch or cowrie was described by my aunt as 'all too Marseilles-matelot for my taste'; while the Brigadier had found nothing amusing in the fact that the proprietor was known to most of his clients as Wild Bill Seafood.)

All this, as I say, returned to me as I followed the

length of bridal veil and its unusual flotsam, my only other thought being a prayer that we would be able to escape without being waylaid by Lord Lovescombe, who was at that moment 'heaving into view', as Victor Crane would have described it. By the desk with the calf-bound book of suggestions for wedding gifts, a largeish crowd had collected, as if in anticipation of Carmen's parodic wedding march; among them a tall man with a mournful expression and a woman roughly half his height, reminding me suddenly, and, as it turned out, accurately, of Lord Lovescombe's remark on one of the occasions of my visiting Amy in London that 'Charles and Lucy Edge are coming to dinner . . . an unsuited couple . . . like the mating of a kangaroo and a cat!' and of Lady Lovescombe's pained demand that her husband should stop being 'disgusting'. That Lord Lovescombe should have chosen this epithet for friends of his had seemed at the time cruel, not to say unnecessary; that it had summed them up unforgettably was borne out by my instant recognition of the ill-assorted pair, even though they had themselves – unless Lord Lovescombe had slyly supplied an equivalent description of me – no idea at all of who I, in return, could be.

Further speculation on this couple was, however, out of the question, due to an extraordinary noise, shrill and cacophonous as a peacock, which now filled the Bridal Department – and went in all probability beyond, even the carefully padded and overstuffed reproduction settees and chairs in the adjoining hall being hardly capable of stifling such a shriek – and the vertiginous figure of Edge, stooping as it was over the list of prescribed wedding gifts, straightened and looked myopically out in the direction of the din. His wife's eyes flashed with a sudden marsupial shrewdness from their position by Charles Edge's lowest-but-one waistcoat button. Lord Loves-combe, firmly retaining his stance behind Nagra Pont's chair, was startled none the less into muttering an oath; while Carmen, relieved I think that some attention had been diverted from her illegal train, increased her speed in the direction of the door to the stairs. She looked back, grabbing my hand so that we gave the appearance – or so I self-consciously thought – of an eloping couple of a persuasion not recognized by Queen Victoria but certainly approved of by Ethel – and gave a short, angry laugh. 'That's Juniper Berry,' she said.

'What do you mean?' We passed the desk guarded by Nagra, now swathed from the waist downward in a swirl of damask patterned with white roses. I wondered if a guest to the Castle Azeby wedding had asked to see the tablecloth and had then, perhaps on grounds of size or expense, decided against buying it. Its abandoned, crumpled state certainly suggested an absence of future hospitality on the part of Amy and her new husband, Crispin Hare, and brought, chilling as so many innocent wedding gift suggestions can be, unstoppable visions of a marital unhappiness – even instant divorce – lying ahead for the couple. I paused, bringing Carmen and her canopy of stolen goods to a sudden halt, and was startled by another rendering of the appalling, ear-shattering dis-cordance.

'Juniper Berry – you must have heard of him, Jenny!' Carmen, satisfied by further confirmation of my social inexpertise, seemed quite prepared now to linger in a position of maximum exposure, where not only the *vendeuses* could see her but also the decrepit experimental novelist himself, who, recently jettisoned by the exasperated saleswomen, was determinedly rerouting himself in the direction of the desk. 'Juniper Berry was carried down the High Street at Oxford in a coffin,' Carmen said delightedly. 'He edited a magazine with Fuck the Pope in it, or something.'

It's hard to describe, at this distance of time, the effect then of the Anglo-Saxon word just triumphantly uttered by Carmen on practically any member of the British public – with the exception, possibly, of what the Brigadier was fond of referring to as 'navvies'. Ignored up to this point in the department, despite the obvious irregularities in her retinue, Carmen immediately became the centre of attention. Lord Lovescombe, 'doting' on Nagra Pont, as J. D. Hare had been loudly and to no one in particular describing the activities of his about-to-be in-law, straightened up and looked severely over in our direction. Charles and Lucy Edge, for whom indeed the word may have carried confusing reverberations, peered out at us from behind a palisade of *dentelle* nighties and nylon-quilted coverlets. A *vendeuse*, hair crisply white as her snowy wares, marched up to Carmen and tapped her on the shoulder. 'Excuse me, young lady. Will you come this way please?'

The next moments, while frantic, saved me in my hopeless quest for napkins for Aunt Babs – and, more to the point, saved me definitively from the attentions of Candida, now bearing down on us fast. The sound of the forbidden obscenity had brought furious colour to her cheeks, though whether, as Carmen later remarked, this was due to the four letters standing as a reminder of past or current 'greens' with Mick Scupper or a genuine desire to help out a pair of old schoolfriends at a time of need was unclear. In her wake, toppling pin-striped and tailed wedding guests in plaster attitudes of congratulation and complacency, came J. D. Hare. Carmen pulled away sharply from our assailant, the avenging saleslady, and tugged at my hand to insist on an urgent getaway by the stairs. The bridal veil, I saw with relief, had become detached from whatever in her porous tights had caught it there – a safety-pin probably – and was now slumped at the *vendeuse*'s feet. True assistance, however, came from an unexpected quarter.

'My dear madam!' A more muffled but distinctly recognizable peacock scream followed these words, the sound this time being clearly intended as an expression of amusement. 'Do you know whom we have here? Incognito, of course, but owing to these unfortunate circumstances necessarily introduced, if only in the strictest confidence –'

The person of Juniper Berry, for this it undoubtedly was, was one more likely to repel than to encourage comment. Curly hair, much frowned on in that age of Brylcreem and hair oil, stood out in a mild bush above a face reminiscent in its uncomfortable, flat-lipped way of both Oscar Wilde and also of late photographs of Edwardian beauties such as Lady Desborough. Most remarkable – and again completely unknown at that time – was the bottle-green suit, sharply tailored to show an elegant body and long, tapering legs, and a matching umbrella, which, as the Oxford reprobate and printed blasphemer furled and unfurled it in the face of the astonished manageress ('very unlucky to open an umbrella indoors' as Ethel's voice irresistibly came back to me) did indeed resemble the fan of a strutting peacock, only too well aware of its ambiguous charms and potency.

Even J. D. Hare, who had, from the signs given out by his wildly twisting mouth, an entire lecture to deliver on the subject of the old English word and its hypocritical repression on the very shores which had given birth to it (a talk to include the evil censorship imposed on James Joyce and the efforts of Sylvia Beach in Paris) was forced into a reluctant silence. I saw Candida, whose Head Girl expression had become more pronounced as she approached, falter and also come to a standstill on the far side of the counter attended by Nagra Pont.

Something uneasy stirred in Candida's features as Juniper Berry spoke; and I must admit myself that the charged atmosphere, the strong sense of illusion produced by the young man with his high, piercing call and odd, slightly mechanical movements, made me think, if only very briefly, that I was once more at St Peter's School for Girls and under the spell of Carmen's latest 'improvisation'. (Candida was, for all her sensible exterior, even more of a 'sucker', as Carmen would gleefully have put it, for special privileges than the rest of us: there was a compelling need in her, I knew, for hierarchy, monarchy, order.)

'. . . none other than Princess Mathilda of Slovenia,' Juniper Berry was saying in a voice harsh now with a different sort of excitement: 'I know, my dear lady, that her Royal Highness Princess Mathilda is planning to attend the Castle Azeby wedding. She is in need of guidance as to which of the items she should purchase for the lucky couple – and I don't mean, I may say, items from the list so efficiently produced by the Right Honourable Baroness Lovescombe for the purpose. No, *ma chère madame*, the Princess wishes to inquire whether a white convertible Rolls-Royce, complete, of course, with leopard-skin picnic-hamper and white satin upholstery, can be ordered in this store and placed on her charge account here.'

For a moment I had to feel sorry for Carmen. She stood – 'boggling' as she later freely admitted – at the sheer nerve of it. Whether she also saw, as I did – and possibly Candida too – her own propensity for 'whoppers' (as the Brigadier had unfailingly described Carmen's explanations of her ancestry on the rare occasions of her coming to tea at Aunt Babs') magnified a hundredfold in the behaviour of Juniper Berry was more questionable. Carmen had, in the days before an alliance with the Stones or the Beatles became the *ne plus ultra*, felt it necessary to produce exotic minor royalty, the odd gypsy, and on one memorable occasion the splitter of the atom, Rutherford, in her pedigree, and had firmly believed it all herself. What she would do in the face of a yarn-spinner even more audacious was hard to say: what did seem to be the case, however, was that the head *vendeuse* in the Bridal Department shared the look of confusion and awe visible on Candida's face – the look which had transported me so effortlessly to St Peter's and to the instant, amused memories of Carmen's tales of spa-dwelling, throneless princes.

'We will take some of the requisites for a honeymoon picnic from this department,' Juniper Berry said hastily, as if a second longer on this particular trail might bring insufferable boredom. 'Aha, what have we here?' And, tugging at the damask tablecloth which still protruded in a swirl from the lower regions of Nagra's desk, freed a cloud of white material which temporarily, as in a séance, obscured the scene altogether. Dimly aware of the rather shocking – because unexpected – sight of Nagra Pont's legs under the desk, I also became aware of Lord Loves-combe's sudden shout of remonstrance, and of Juniper Berry's hand slipping over my wrist. He held something soft; I was made to take hold of the bundle; after this came a sharp nudge in the rear and the peacock scream, a little muted this time, as we made at speed for the door. 'My bridesmaid,' Juniper Berry explained me over his shoulder in his raucous tones as we at last reached the exit and stone stairs beyond. 'Now for the buying of the dear little chunky Rolls!'

We raced down, leaving behind the stunned patrons of the Bridal Department. These formed a group of almost Hogarthian consternation and dismay, in which the out-flung arms of Lord Lovescombe had alighted, not on the young siren Nagra on her rock in the sea of grey pile carpet, but on Candida Tarn, who in turn stood mouth agape as if undergoing the breaking of a powerful taboo. While Charles and Lucy Edge, like courtiers at a panto-mime court, tried to prevent J. D. Hare from following us at breakneck speed down the stairs.

Unseemly visions of missing marriage settlements, un-settled futures, promises of a broker's life for the groom now broken, gathered force as we plunged down away from the chamber of vows. Matrimony, on our staircase, was succeeded by alimony, a whole steppe of furs opening out before us on the second floor, and it was only as we reached the celibate sobriety of Gents Outfitters that

Juniper Berry paused and permitted himself another fainter, dying shriek.

'My dear Carmen,' he said as we took breath for a moment in the uniforms for Haileybury, Oundle and Marlborough, 'thank you for introducing me to your charming friend. She looks so magnificently shocked!' And, pushing the bundle of damask napkins with which he had christened me bridal attendant to the Princess of Slovenia into the depths of the carry-all provided by Aunt Babs as a suitable receptacle for honestly acquired merchandise of a similar description, he blew us both a kiss and skipped through the pillars of Perfumery out into Hans Place.

CHAPTER FIVE

'Picasso? Yes, grossly overrated. One has to be careful about what one says when staying with Douglas, he's more touchy than ever. But the rooms of Braque and Juan Gris are pretty well done, I must admit.'

The speaker, a man of about forty-five, was at first screened from me in the crowded saloon bar of the Bunch of Grapes by the swaying bodies of, amongst others, Victor Crane and J. D. Hare – who seemed, despite differences of approach to the problems of the world, to be magnetically attracted to each other in some way: almost as if the two men, like people in a sketch in one of the 'revues' still fashionable at that time, knew they represented an era, the 'Thirties', and, sensing a new wave of artistic protest afoot (Lord Lovescombe was at that very moment complaining of the 'angries' he considered to be patronizing the pub), clung together to remind their audience of Auden, the Spanish Civil War and Leon Trotsky. Comparisons with Picasso's *Guernica*, known to me as a result of Aunt Babs' cousins the Stringers' determination to educate me in the arts on each occasion of their visits to London – it being otherwise only too easy to stay

94

within the confines of Portobello Road and the studio where I learnt to gild the mirrors and console tables of our customers – would not have been inapposite when describing the scene I had just walked into. The Bunch of Grapes, a pub in a mews behind Harrods, was a rendezvous clearly well known to Carmen and was already the haunt of a large, anguished clientele. J. D. Hare, detaching himself from the swaying figures, could now be seen to be bearing in each hand an iceless, lemonless, colourless glass which betokened, in those days (and unchangingly, still betokens) English gin and tonic: his face, empurpled by the heat and smoke of the place, resembling a kipper or a dark, Basque ham hung up to dry in the lofters of a French farmhouse kitchen, the last image being only recently available to us as the recipes of Elizabeth David and the post-war longing for France ('French flu', as Ethel called it) gripped Bohemia and the upper middle classes of the epoch. The change of stance of the writer and about-to-be father-in-law released a view of a corner of the banquette where the unseen speaker was sitting, and, picking up the last shouted remark from that quarter, J. D. Hare appeared to decide on a gallant attempt to 'bring in' the younger generation – in this case, after one look at Carmen's hostile, sarcastic expression, myself.

'I expect you know Jim Tremlett, Jenny.' Hare, with great difficulty, set down the two glasses on the table overflowing with ashtrays, empty beer mugs and crisps packets. 'He's been staying near Avignon with Douglas Cooper. You know the . . . art expert . . . you know . . .'

The fact that I didn't in no way deflected me from a sense of discomfiture, alarm almost, on seeing Jim Trem-

95

lett; and it was in some ways a relief to realize that I was as thoroughly forgotten by him, since the disastrous weekend several years before at Lovegrove, as, say, a passenger on the same train down to Salisbury might have been. Tremlett, editor of *Margin* (which had, in the intervening years, 'folded', according to Ethel when asked later if she still sold back issues of the journal), and, most memorably, husband of Jasmine Tremlett, whom I had, to my eternal shame and within earshot of Lord Lovescombe, described as a 'tart' on that same weekend, still had the seedy look – hair, elbows, knees in ancient flannels, as I recalled, all slightly shiny and somehow transparent-looking – the only difference as far as I could make out being an increase in the dark, 'smoked' complexion clearly a professional hazard to those who frequented such places. Intimations of exposure to hell-fire, or at least a recent roasting, lent a hint of evil to the retired literary editor as he peered out at me through a cloud of smoke from his Senior Service.

'You say we've met before? You the girl who sent in that erotic story?'

J. D. Hare gave a loud chuckle before I had time to answer. 'No, no, Jim, that's Lady Nell. One of the Filtrinchams. At Oxford – you met her when we went down for the evening on Logical Positivism, remember?'

The memory of the evening seemed to set off no pleasant reverberations, for Tremlett put his head in his hands, thus grazing and sending almost immediately to the floor an array of pint mugs on the crowded table in front of him. The sound of breaking glass brought a sudden hush to the pub, and it was all the more painfully possible to hear voices in the cobbled mews outside. An elderly man, resembling more a toad than one of the 'kippered' inmates of the Bunch of Grapes, threaded his way through to where Tremlett, apparently unmoved by the breakage, still sat invisible behind his hands. The landlord, equally interested in reaching Tremlett, pushed with less ceremony from the raised flap of the bar.

'That was one hell of an evening,' the toad-like man remarked, as the hubbub slowly started up again. 'You know what?' He turned to me, eyes darting with a frequency that was this time reminiscent of the movements of a lizard's tail. A claw-like hand came out, as if to complete this prehensile personality, the talons digging into my arm. 'Branff. Allow me to introduce myself. Francis Branff,' he let out on what was now a necessarily high note. 'You're a friend of Lady Nell's too, I expect?'

'Of course she is!' Tremlett, as suddenly as he had hidden his face, now unmasked himself. The 'rumpus', as the Brigadier would undoubtedly have referred to it, was less audible in the mews now, partly as a result of the din in the interior; a loud, chanting sound could nevertheless be made out.

'Francis is our most important philosopher,' J. D. Hare said with a loud snigger, just behind me. 'I heard about the evening in Oxford, by the way. Absolute scandal, I must say.'

'It wouldn't have been so bad if Victor hadn't insisted on turning up with a bottle of booze,' Tremlett said. 'What was the question, Branff, from the audience – "What would you say, if a vehicle, gathering velocity at x per second, was coming down the hill . . ."'

'"I'd say shit", is exactly what you said,' Francis Branff replied with pleasure. 'Worthy of Comrade Victor himself.' And, as Crane, drawn despite his repudiation of the status of the individual to the sound of his own name, made his way towards us, the small, reptilian philosopher let out a gravelly laugh. 'Crane claims to know the lovely Lady Nell,' he barked. 'Whether in the biblical sense or not we cannot ascertain. Through your connection with the last of the bright and beautiful, the Lovescombes. Isn't that right, Victor?'

'So far as I know,' Crane said, with a surprising stiffness I thought, as if the discussion of lineage had long ago been circumscribed and would now probably carry a penalty, 'the Filtrinchams are not connected with the Lovescombe family in any way.'

'She's got a filthy mind, whoever she is,' Tremlett said, with a gleeful conspiratorial glance which included and seemed for a moment to implicate me. 'You're in disguise,' he added in my direction, as a perfunctory search in the breast pocket of his worn tweed jacket had clearly failed to come up with the proof in manuscript of Lady Nell's profanity. 'That's Lady Nell in drag, Victor!'

The need to get out had now once again become paramount; besides this I saw Carmen fighting her way to the door; and the combination of the promise of fresh air and the possibility of getting away from this 'low crowd' (the Brigadier), 'Britain's foremost intellectuals' (Ethel), was too tempting to forgo. I pushed past the table where Jim Tremlett was sitting and on through the crowd to the shaft of light, clouded with smoke, that came in through the open door.

'Kicked me in the groin – that's a girl.' It was possible to hear Tremlett's voice, raised in mock pain, right up to the last pockets of drinking, crushed people. And I

98

thought, as I finally reached a pillar of doubtful light and fought my way on to the cobbles, that I'd had enough for one day. The carry-all, no doubt one of the causes of Tremlett's agony, still held the purloined napkins and should be taken back to Harrods; and the whole surreal sequence of events explained away as best as possible. Or, I should simply go home and confess the whole episode to Aunt Babs. I knew, as Carmen waved to me in the relative freedom of the mews beyond the door of the public house, that I would end up doing this. Although it was more likely that the thief of a Chelsea dove would advise me on neither course, pointing out the preferable nature of returning with the napkins at the end of the day and handing them to my aunt as if they had been purchased – while at the same time profiting from the money handed over for that purpose.

Once out in the air, I had the choice of turning left, waving goodbye to Carmen and making my way down to the Scotch House and thence to the 52 bus which would take me close to the Portobello Road, or of going over to talk to her; and it was with some sense of restored dignity that I decided on the former. It was getting late, and, napkins apart, Aunt Babs would be concerned about possible coming disasters at the fund-raising dinner that evening, not the least of these being her reasonable dread of Lady Pickering, a generous donor but 'stuffy', and, in my aunt's eyes, unlikely to appreciate the tepid chicken vol-au-vent mysteriously always produced for such an occasion of social precariousness, the flimsy pastry cases, brimming with a mushy mixture and too awkward to be eaten standing at a buffet dinner, resembling the state of my poor aunt's own innards and fragile outer case. The Stringers, too, with their expectations of a cuisine certainly not available at that time in Britain, would be likely to draw attention to the poor fare on offer, if only unintentionally; and for all my desire to get more information from Carmen on the subject of Amy's wedding, and the possible relationships of Amy and Scupper, or Scupper and Candida (we hadn't met since the afternoon spent in Nagra Pont's flat in Rossetti Gardens Mansions, the announced insubstantiality of the place matched by the confused, drug-induced memories I had of that time) I determined to walk away from such temptation as quickly as possible. Carmen's lurid tales, whether of Amy's pregnancy or of the 'tegover' of Hare, Lovescombe and Rudd, as she described in her imitations of 'Bluey' and others, could be gone into when my aunt's dinner was safely in the past. Besides, I had had enough fantasy for the day. Juniper Berry, outdoing even Carmen in his proclamations of her ancestry, had returned me – and Candida, too, as I had briefly seen – to that moment between childhood and adulthood when any 'story', particularly if reminiscent of the historical romances enjoyed by girls of that period – Violet Needham, say, or Margaret Irwin – seems plausible. I had no wish any longer, as I made off at a brisk pace in the direction of Knightsbridge, to concern myself wondering about Ludo and Candida. The romance, for me, was over, Candida had 'won'. The brief glimpse I had had of guests and relatives gathered together in the Bridal Department of Harrods would suffice me when it came to the Lovescombes and their family and hangers-on, for a long time to come. Life as normal – although I didn't like to look too closely at what this really held out for me – could resume from now. I hadn't even the slightest inclination, as I told myself with a new feeling of lightness and self-understanding, of going to the wedding at Castle Azeby. The combination of farce and cruelty associated in my mind when it came to con-templating the Lovescombes and their entourage had been suffered already at Lovegrove; while the predictable unpredictabilities of Carmen had succeeded in preventing me from getting anything to wear for the wretched event. I felt richer, too, at the thought of going without an outfit that would in all probability never be worn again; and, reminding myself that I owed little allegiance to Amy by now – for in all her vigils abroad while waiting to reach the age of marriage she had hardly once re-membered me – I reached the imposing corner building which, window-dressed as it was with tartans, heather and plaid, seemed uncomfortably close to that northern home of Amy's which I had no longer any desire to visit.

I paused by the shop's curved window at the juncture of two thoroughfares and looked in at the knitwear dis-play. I might buy myself a cardigan. Or – possibly – a twinset, emblem of luxury and 'spoiltness' to my aunt, whose contempt for the Royal Family, as far as I could make out, stemmed mainly from their wearing of these harmless matching garments.

Perusal of the window, scattered 'tastefully' with grouse claws and autumn leaves (as Aunt Babs, mild in all things but matters of taste, used the adjective in verbal quotes to show an almost violent loathing of pretension, of an affectation of 'taste'), was not to last long, however; not in peace, at least. The first intimation that I was not alone came from the unsubtle, if unmistakable, gesture with which I would always connect the French, since the occasion of a visit for cultural purposes with the Stringers to Paris the year before; the only difference being, as I could see from the reflection in the plate-glass window, that my assailant, despite the fact of wearing a beret, was certainly not French. I must have stepped back sharply, I suppose, for the deliverer of the insulting gesture gave a startled shout; while in the background, supplying a kind of dismal bagpipes to this unscheduled jig, came the sound of the chant I had heard outside the Bunch of Grapes in the mews behind Harrods. I turned, to find myself looking down on the mushroom stalk of a beret – jowls and a bulbous nose just visible beneath suggested an attempt to emulate Picasso – and, as memories of a troll-sized bathroom at Lovegrove returned to me, so too did an uneasy memory of keyhole spying, or something very near it, on the first, nerve-shattering evening of Amy's parents' hospitality. Before I could move further away – a 52 bus was visible at that moment and I could have jumped on it if I had been free – my hand was clasped in a grip as Gallic as the rest.

'My dear girl! I didn't recognize you!' Walter Neet looked up at me with an air of ferocious apology, leaving me to work out whether this lack of recognition was intended as a compliment, given the outrageous action just perpetrated, or an admission that I, in his eyes – as at the time of our original meeting – was hardly worth the pressure of finger and thumb. Before I had time to ponder this, Neet, as if joining me in some form of un-welcome telepathy, gave a loud snort of laughter.

'That was a fairly frantic weekend,' he said. 'And we met again at the Lovescombes' ball, did we not? Yes,

yes.' He stopped, eyes clouding over in a now recognizable attack of self-acclaim, the very severity of which
enabled me to remove my crushed fingers from his clasp.
'You were admiring my paintings in that room off the
top landing, weren't you? Ludo's room, I believe. Oh my
goodness, yes. They hang them high up there for the
light, you know. Old Lovers told me himself. "I don't
mind putting those ghastly, dim Gainsboroughs and Van
Dycks in the ground-floor rooms where there's never any
light," Richard Lovescombe said to me. "But yours,
Walter, need the marvellous feeling of fresh air, of –".'
Neet's arms swept out in an arc, nearly knocking an
Indian student – or so the duffle coat and knapsack of
books on his back suggested – off the pavement and into
the flow of traffic. 'The sheer scope of Castle Azeby,'
Walter Neet continued loudly, as the young overseas
visitor, with an expression of surprise followed by in-
credulity, looked closer at Neet. 'You're going to Castle
Azeby, my dear Jenny, I take it? Going on the old train?'
For a moment Neet's eyes darkened. 'Least they could
have done is offer to pay one's ticket, don't you agree?
Even if there is free champagne.' And, seeing me falter
before embarking on an answer, he added suddenly:
'Unless you're driving, dear girl. Got a car by now, I dare-
say?'

The assumption that a car, along with other manifestations, such as a developed 'bust' for instance – an appellation on which Aunt Babs insisted, scorning the word
'bra' even at the risk of going misunderstood in the department stores when asking for a 'bust bodice' – had
become automatically mine on reaching maturity prevented me from explaining to Walter Neet that I had no

103

intention of going to Castle Azeby at all, whatever the type of conveyance. The chanting sounds, now identifiable as a plea for nuclear disarmament, had become closer too as we stood in the fork of the road outside the Scotch House; and I saw, as the retinue approached, that Leopold Tarn was the bearer of the banner, while Carmen, not surprisingly, had tagged along. Nagra Pont was at her side in one of the new sheepskin coats for which I knew Carmen had a penchant. A couple of young people in donkey jackets, with fringes and a depressed air – deserving doubtless in Lord Lovescombe's eyes the epithet 'spotty'– made up the rest of the cortège; and to the side of them, but very much not of them, as her aloof and contemptuous expression made clear, came Candida. A large Harrods carrier-bag proclaimed her status as a shopper rather than a disarmer – a position, as I was able to reflect grimly many years later, that was underlined with hideous irony at the time of the bombing of the store, Carmen just as now, not far away.

'Good Lord, there's that girl.' Neet stared greedily at Carmen, reminding me of his declaration of love for her before lunch at the time of our visit to Lovegrove. 'And there – Candida, isn't it? Candida Tarn?'

I said it was, though the placing of Candida by Neet so effortlessly only led me back to those very thoughts I had so lately forbidden myself: the question of whom Candida would shortly become. Memories of the proprietorial air adopted by her towards Castle Azeby, as represented in the collection of Walter Neet's watercolours hanging in Ludo's room in Regent's Park, and thus towards Ludo himself, seemed dimly to return to the artist as he stared at the procession making its way towards the flying buttress of the Scotch House. 'Candida – yes. Didn't she suggest pulling down that appalling loggia added in the twenties? Good taste, that girl. One would have to paint the place all over again, of course, if it were to go. But that's life, I suppose.'

The thought of added commissions at Castle Azeby having presumably removed any other associations of Candida and Ludo from his mind – or, more horribly, it being so taken for granted that Candida would be the next mistress of the house – Neet returned his attentions to Carmen, by now the wearer of the sheepskin, while Nagra, denuded as she had been so suddenly of her lower covering at the desk in the Bridal Department – a natural victim, perhaps, of the greed or random misbehaviour of whoever happened to be in the vicinity – marched bravely on in a white cardigan and thin looking skirt. Neet clapped his hands in admiration of Carmen's new, shaggy appearance, and I had to admit, even while trying to figure out my way back across the park to Bayswater in an attempt to evade both of the Tarns, that there was something magnificent, almost mythical about her. Beauty with the body of a beast, she seemed to have metamorphosed directly from the loins of an avenging goddess, or from the pages of an Arthur Crane picture book. She saw me and waved; and over the plangent demands to ban the bomb came a call that I should go with her to Nagra's for tea. Neet, pricking up his ears at this, stepped forward and extended a hand. A group of pedestrians, already dislodged by the protest group, swore in an unidentifiable Scandinavian language at the small bereted figure.

Carmen detached herself from Leopold Tarn's small

army and came over to us. Near to, the frizz of hair and dark ringed eyes over an expanse of white woolly pelt gave a gentler appearance, as if she had in fact transmogrified into one of the flock tended by a poetic shepherd, Daphnis perhaps, who had not long before undergone the inductions into love initiated by the old nurse on the arrival of Chloe. This obvious increase on Carmen's part in worldly knowledge and experience in no way deterred Walter Neet from his determination to go on where he had, so to speak, left off four years before: if anything, as I realized with one of the twinges of surprise still only too often suffered at eighteen, it only made him all the more determined to 'have his way with her' – as Ethel's more unsalubrious titles would undoubtedly delineate his intentions. Neet's eyes, matched in angry puffiness by the boils and pustules of almost Job-like dimensions on his cheeks and lurching neck, came close to popping out of his head altogether at the sight of Carmen as female satyr, many-profiled in her reflections in the plate-glass windows of the Scotch House; and, as if making a life decision to abandon water-colour sketches of architectural views in favour of exotic studies, he held an imaginary palette aloft in one hand, the other eagerly embracing the form of Carmen with an equally illusory brush.

'Carmen!' Neet now approached at speed, making a dangerous clash with the disarmers almost inevitable. I could see Candida draw up, by now, and frown in dim recognition of the little artist; while Leo, clearly ignored by his sister in his efforts to put an end to the arms race, braked within a few feet of her. Neet, running at full speed and with flapping raincoat, had quite disrupted both civilian and political life in this stretch of Knightsbridge.

'My dear Carmen, I invite you to the Academy Cinema followed by a small repast in my studio,' Neet shouted. 'I do hope you will agree. A French film . . . *La Règle du Jeu* . . .'

Carmen, as I had to remind myself later in that strenuous and unexpected day, was not only capable of appearing in multiple guises – indeed, like Picasso's many-faceted women, she could be seen as saint and sinner, harlot and madonna, bluestocking and sorceress all in one – but could wreak transformations, sometimes, it had to be admitted, of the most sadistic kind, on her fellow human beings. A roar of sudden and appreciative laughter went up from the crowd, brought to a standstill anyway by the cross-currents of Leo's band. A driver shouted from a 22 bus, blocked in its attempt to gain entry to Sloane Street; and for a moment, as if a witch exercising her powers was as commonplace as the signals of a policeman on traffic duty, we all saw what Carmen intended us to see: a world of fairy-tale illustration, a vision as comic as it was malevolent: Neet as a scurrying chipmunk, with beret and plumed, cartoon tail; Candida, pale as a wax princess, among her subjects a throng of woodland denizens; Leo a blond bear, draped in his banner like the pelt of a slain adversary; and Nagra, trotting beside him, as bugsy-eyed as a bunny in a bedtime story.

I was grateful for this chance to escape at last, my plan to slip off in the direction of Hyde Park having become finally possible; and as Carmen stood laughing down at Walter Neet from within her shaggy coat, I did just that, closing my ears to the sound of my name as it was increasingly loudly called out – the sound, indeed, to my embarrassment, seeming to outdo even the resumed pleas to put an end to the hydrogen bomb.

'Jenny!' Another voice, this time definitely unknown to me, came breathlessly at my back. 'This *is* Jenny Carter, I take it?'

Again the intonations were unusual. I stopped and turned, protected now by the looming shape of the Scotch House from Carmen and Neet as well as from the incompatible combination of Candida Tarn and her brother, the one so neatly and perfectly dressed (as if for the wedding at Castle Azeby already, I had caught myself thinking with a burst of spite, a single row of pearls at the neck and the undoubted intimation of a silk shirt under a 'fitted' coat) and the other so roughly garbed, as if foretelling already in his dress the end of civilization after the bomb. This wasn't the grating voice of Neet – nor that of Lord Lovescombe, had he chased out of Harrods in his pursuit of Nagra Pont. Some of the careful English of the editor of *Margin*, Jim Tremlett, was there, possibly, but the voice was too deliberate and mellifluous for his – and too low-pitched and thoughtful to belong to those accustomed to slur, spit and stutter like J.D. Hare and Victor Crane. A hand, light but curiously insistent, tugged my sleeve from behind. 'Excuse me – I have been told you will take me to your aunt.'

I certainly had to stop at this and turn round. The Indian student, for he it was, stood in the relative peace of the pavement facing Knightsbridge Barracks. As if in an imperial postcard of the late nineteenth century, the sun set behind the red brick of the monstrous building and engulfed us both in a sudden post-colonial gloom. Before I had time to wonder how I could have been tracked down in this way, identified even, by a total stranger only newly arrived on these shores, the young visitor started to explain the sequence of events which had directed him towards me.

'I am a correspondent of Leopold Tarn.' A gleam in the eye suggested long, political news-sheets rather than the chatty musings of a pen pal. 'I am going up to Oxford next week, where of course Leopold is editor of *Left Journal*. Until then I have nowhere to stay, as my brother, who was expecting me, has been transferred to Birmingham.' The small hand, light but if anything more placatory and insistent than before, settled delicately on my arm. 'Leopold's sister – I believe it was she to whom I was introduced just now –'

'Candida,' I said, hearing myself sound grim.

'Yes, Candida. Very charming. She told me Leo was a good friend of yours – it was impossible to speak to him, of course, on the march – and that you had so very kindly arranged for my accommodation in London. I understand you are in Notting Hill. I have just been reading the extremely interesting books of Colin MacInnes on the subject of the West Indian community in London.'

The sudden, unbidden thought that this was not the first of Candida's recent manipulative manoeuvres as far as I was concerned prevented me from replying immediately. There had been an odd cageyness in Amy's voice when ringing to discuss 'wedding plans', and she had apologized for the fact that I was to be stationed out, about four miles from Castle Azeby, 'staying with the Cleggs'. Now perhaps, by parking a stranger on me, Candida had decided in view of my obvious attraction to Ludo as witnessed at the Lovescombe ball, to stop me going altogether. But now a youth, identifiable as a member of Leo's contingent, could be seen racing up from the passage leading to Knightsbridge Green, arms waving and banner trailing, as if the recovery of my companion had become all at once of far greater consequence than the scrapping of the bomb.

'Hey!' The youth, avoiding my smile and greeting, went straight up to the Indian student and stood in front of him. A name, inaudible to me because of a loud churning from what appeared to be a line of giant cement mixers in the street, was said and agreed to. Together, the two young men made their way back, down in the direction of the Hyde Park Hotel, where Leo, now surrounded by policemen, could just be glimpsed. The student paused for a moment by me. 'Please give my apologies to your aunt.' Seeing Candida at the far end of a small shopping-arcade, he waved, and receiving no salute in reply, looked sadly down for a moment. 'It appears that I am to be billeted with Leopold Tarn himself,' he said. 'There was a misunderstanding. My apologies once more.'

I felt for a moment that to stay with the Tarns, an experience I had undergone while at St Peter's – the most memorable occasion being our severely punished jaunt, the attempt to get to the Lovescombes' midsummer ball – might be more than the newly-arrived undergraduate had bargained for. I almost suggested that he come home with me to Aunt Babs' after all. Only the thought of my aunt's exasperation, and the impending dinner party which in turn reminded me of the contraband napkins I was due to take to her – stopped me from this; while Candida's slow and hostile approach along the arcade in our direction sent Leo's new friend shuffling off at some speed to join him. He would have enough of Candida later, as perhaps he had guessed; and I thought of how hopelessly divided the Tarn household must be by now, with an activist – and active pacifist – under the same roof as a conservative such as Candida, whose name was inscribed at last on the roll of honour at St Peter's for scholastic achievements, a scholarship to Oxford, the Head Girlship, which – so Amy had gigglingly told me – had predictably been conferred on her after a certain amount of discreet politicking. The very aura of law and order which surrounded Candida would madden Leo, I thought – and would probably lead him, before the year was out, to full-scale anarchy. (That I was wrong in this: that a more brutal totalitarianism was to overtake his character than anything – at that point, at least – which could grow in Candida, I could not at that time have wildly guessed.)

There followed what I could only later think of as a prophetic and disturbing succession of events, the first being the appearance at the far end of the paved walk of Amy and Crispin Hare, and the second, following close after, of Ludo and his and Amy's mother, Lady Lovescombe. A glass shop was obviously their destination; the four bunched together – as if just emerging from or about to enter the portals of a church, as it suddenly looked to me – and Candida, expression changing from one of extreme aggression (at the sight of the now banished Indian student) to frank grumpiness at the sight of myself, turned with a rapt smile towards the party. Unseeing, the young couple, if the bride and groom-to-be could be so described, continued to make their way into the shop. Candida called out a greeting. The Lovescombe family showed no sign of hearing her. They went single file into the tiny shop. Candida, about to follow them with eagerness, stopped in her tracks and frowned. Then, aware I suppose that I was watching her, she assumed almost an air of swagger and marched in after them.

'What is so terribly funny is that the little red-eyed mice look so exactly like the bridesmaids,' Lady Lovescombe was saying as I, driven this time by a sort of foolhardiness that came (or so I pretended) from the knowledge that I was free of all of them in my decision to stay in London and get on with my life, found myself half-way down from the arcade and walking in behind them. 'I mean those awful little Pont girls, one had always thought of them as a litter . . . and look, Amy darling, do look, this plump little songbird, or whatever it is, isn't it absolutely the spitting image of Nell Filtrincham?'

'We're buying presents for the bridesmaids, Jenny,' Ludo said in a quiet amused tone after seeing me. 'Now what would you recommend for the best man? That's me by the way.'

'Oh, this lovely glass tiger,' Candida said shrilly, from a position close up against Ludo and his mother and almost toppling a cabinet of finger-bowls, water-lily shaped, thinner than a soap bubble. 'Tiger, tiger, burning bright,' she added, voice deliberately lowered this time, and strangely breathy. 'Just look at his burning eyes!'

'I expect they'd rather get money,' Amy said in a dull voice. Then she looked straight across at me, and I saw she had been crying. 'Oh let's get it over with.' She held out two minuscule ballerinas, transparent but for the pale dragée-tint tutu and glass slippers like dwarf sickle moons. 'Aren't they *sweet*?' she said in a voice so loaded with misery and sarcasm that it would hardly have been surprising if that very tone of despair had cracked the glass in the shop altogether; 'the Pont twins can put them on their mantelpiece. And how about this for Nagra?' Amy pointed to a swan, gliding glassily over a shelf of glass, so that the shadow, in the beam of the strong showcase light, made a double pattern below. 'Don't you think Nagra is very like a swan, Mummy?'

As if the air, already gelid around the family group, had suddenly reached freezing point, Lady Lovescombe pulled a mink scarf closer to her throat and bared her teeth in what could have been a vulpine snarl or an expression of intense joviality. I wondered why Amy, always disturbed, as I remembered, by her father's affairs with other women, should have chosen to mention Nagra at this point – if Nagra was even reciprocating Lord Lovescombe's feelings, of course – but was only able to receive the message, on a deeper level than speech or gesture, that it was marriage that was a mockery, for Amy: that there was no such thing as love, a fact her parents, throughout her childhood, had amply demonstrated to her; and that to celebrate the farcical institution by, amongst other things, giving a token of gratitude to a bridal attendant who was also very possibly in the train of quite another romance with the patriarch himself, was even more farcical still. I saw in the folded

113

wings of the swan, whitened in that uneven way that glass takes white, a complicit understanding between the girl and Lady Lovescombe, and that Amy was afraid of it, wanted it exposed and banished at the same time – and I saw how her fear of these arrangements, instilled at an early age when witnessing the cynicism, brittle as glass itself, of mother and father, had led her to prefer flight or break-up to the endless, cloying lies. The swan, picked suddenly and clumsily off the shelf by Amy, was handed to the shop assistant. 'I want it gift-wrapped, like in America,' Amy said. And, to my horror wept quite openly, if silently, as the beak of the glass bird and its now visible black-web stockings and yellow glass feet went upside down into a cardboard box and a cloud of fine tissue paper.

'Look at this!' Candida said in a loud voice, commanding and peremptory this time, so that – and I don't think I exaggerate – a ray of the future, of her position of domination over all of us – did indeed shine out refracted by the emporium of glass. 'This giraffe, Lady Lovescombe! Don't you think it's absolutely exactly like Harold Macmillan?'

There was, I thought, more of a resemblance between the Lovescombe family and the whole icy collection than with any public figure – or even with 'the Pont twins' or Nagra Pont herself. Even to be connected in the most remote way with this dynasty of Edwardian power and wealth was to stray into the animal kingdom. And this place where their glassy representations were laid out for sale, was where they recognized themselves. Their indifference to Amy's red eyes and obvious unhappiness could be explained this way, for happiness or unhappiness had nothing to do with settlements, rites, inheritance, succession: indeed, as I saw – and shuddered at seeing it – those red eyes could, for all they cared, have, like the mice's, been made of glass.

Neither Crispin Hare, who appeared to be browsing in a slender gallery leading off the shop – sugary prints could be glimpsed, of Italian campaniles, cypresses and the like – nor Ludo did anything more than stand still – as still as a hare would, say, or a fox, scenting trouble in the wind, waiting for further traces of gunfire or pounding hooves. Candida started to ask Amy about some of the wedding arrangements, and Amy pushed past her to the threshold of the shop. She looked down slightly at me – she must have grown in some of her Continental wanderings, as if by doing this she was at least proving the passing of time – and for a moment I saw agony in her face. 'Jenny, I'm such a rotten failure,' she said, her voice suddenly lighter, making me think more of the taunting, sometimes cruel way in which she would talk of others at school – but this time applying the tone, dangerously, as I came to understand, to herself. She took my arm and led me out of the shop. We stood for a moment in the mugginess of the cramped little arcade, shut off by the glass door that had swung shut behind us. Awkwardly – more as if it were she, rather than Nagra Pont, who was the swan, and, finding it hard at first to walk away from the glassy water, the play of light and shadow, on to dry land – Amy pulled me after her on to the width of the pavement in Brompton Road and the roaring traffic beyond.

'I'm coming to stay with you, Jenny,' she said. 'I mean, can I? Do you mind if I do?'

CHAPTER SIX

The Stringers had already made their mark on my aunt's house by the time Amy and I – after a necessarily silent trip on public transport and in streets washed with hurrying people and falling leaves – had gone down Portobello Road from Notting Hill, and turned left into the narrow street north of Blenheim Crescent where my aunt had lived ever since I could remember. Filled with children, the houses with windowsills crumbling from long neglect, where pots of dying cacti sat as precariously as a clown's crockery on a pole, Scudamore Road had a long way to go before being called 'colourful', an epithet at that time only considered applicable to old Chelsea. A wave of West Indian immigrants had recently arrived, and their fruit and vegetables gave the market an operatic air, as if a set were under construction for a film ('one of those new foreign films', as the Brigadier had it) and certainly not an Ealing comedy; but there was on the whole an atmosphere of hard work, seriousness, making ends meet in houses leaking with cold and rust and sagging appliances. I could see from Amy's face, as she looked about her, that the atmosphere conjured up of raffia-roofed open markets, of heat and spices and a strip of sand where rotting fish had been thrown out not a palm's length away (a sense encouraged by squid and shark on the fishmonger's slab and the sight of the bursting cheeks of water melon and pumpkin cut for Halloween) had changed since the last time Amy had been here, when we were at school together and before this influx of brightness and despair.

I thought, too, as Amy walked with her nervous, slightly jaunty walk, of the air of instability and uncertainty she gave off, in comparison with these tenants of relentless landlords: that the walls of Lovegrove and the doubtless even thicker walls of Castle Azeby had failed to prop her up, to support her at all, even, in the expected way; and that her pallor, together with her hair, longer and less lustrous than it had been in the times I had seen her between 'finishing schools', gave an impression of sadness, even of neglect. There were a good many questions, obviously, that I wanted to ask Amy: about what had happened between her and Mick Scupper, about her future as Mrs Crispin Hare which loomed so improbably near, and how she saw it – but the basic problem, for me, as we walked on in a companionable silence I had almost forgotten was possible between us, was how I could explain my decision not to go to the wedding at all. The Stringers, I had decided on the way down the hill, must be my excuse; and in a tone which I already knew sounded self-conscious, I lurched into an explanation of the special needs of my Aunt Babs' guests and cousins: needs which were real enough but which in their expositions sounded suspiciously like badly concocted reasons for letting Amy down on her wedding day.

117

'What do you mean, you have to look after them and take them to galleries?' Amy said as we reached a relatively quiet stretch of pavement just before my aunt's house. 'Are they arty, or something?'

I must admit that I thought for a moment then and there of doing worse than simply 'chucking' Amy's wedding – as Roly Marr would disapprovingly phrase it, he being a stickler for etiquette – and of telling Amy that it was after all impossible for her to come in to my aunt's. The contrast between her background and expectations and that of the Stringers – not to mention my Aunt Babs, who had been deprived of a view of Amy since she was a schoolgirl – was too great. It was alarming, too, to think – though I didn't, until much later – that all the education, in Florence, Paris, Munich, if education it could be called, had hardly permeated Amy at all. In those very cities where the Stringers lived and painted and played their musical instruments and talked of psychoanalysis and philosophy, Amy had been as a blind person, deaf-mute as well. I wondered, but again only when my own ignorance on these matters became clear to me some years later, whether the walls of Amy's family's various estates had at least done this for her: that she should believe there was nothing outside England of any interest whatsoever; that the boundaries and enclosures of the land still held by such families – and there were still many – could be crossed and hospitality dispensed, while the treasures there were as securely ignored as if they had been old boots in the hall; and that any person outside this concentric ring of philistine enchantment who showed interest in them must automatically be known as 'arty'. I felt sorry for Amy then, and all the more keen to refuse another dose of her particular kind of fascinating dullness. I thought of the libraries of fine books, embossed with the gold crests of French statesmen and the *ancien régime*; the china aviary at Lovegrove, delicate and brittle in alcoves specially built for the purpose; the logs from the great oaks that smouldered in heraldic fireplaces and were dragged in by men whose whole house, granted them in return for the fulfilling of such tasks, could also be fitted snugly in a distant hall. And I thought again that for all my compassion for Amy's recent tears, strange, dejected manner and general air of disaffectedness from the world around her, that I would spare the Stringers the bewilderment of being seen in her particular way by a member of such a family. Amy had her world; a world where her father, as I remembered with the sinking of the heart that comes with the excavation of a forgotten insult, had been heard in my presence to ask Amy, at the time of my visit to Lovegrove, if my aunt was a 'weirdo'. So Amy should stay in her world, a world where news of 'beatniks' and Black Mountain poetry and bead necklaces and 'grass' were the stuff of family jokes. The compound was secure: they had, as Victor Crane had so pertinently pointed out at the lunch before our mass expulsion from Lovegrove, 'the beef and the bullets' to continue to wage an invisible and successful war against the changes in the outside world.

'We do have a bath in our house, actually,' I said. (For I knew, too, that all those who 'dabbled' in the arts, as Lord Lovescombe would term it – that he was a collector of art was quite a different matter – were branded, like those dabblers of the occult arts in bygone days, witches, with being 'dirty'; and unlikely, unless subjected to the ultimate test, to take to water.) Then I burst out laughing at the look of surprise on Amy's face – laughter rapidly succeeded by remorse on my own part at the blow I had clearly dealt her – and led her across the street, away from Aunt Babs' house. 'Let's go and have a coffee first,' I said. 'There are too many people in there – that's all I meant, Amy. We really must talk.'

CHAPTER SEVEN

There are some periods in life which, frozen in their awfulness, seem to have been submerged from sight – possibly for ever – and which, when they do return, are as painful by reason of the flood of memories they release as the part of character relentlessly illumined by the thaw: in my case, a fatal stubbornness or laziness: an inability to face facts, tell the truth and thus spare a great many people a good deal of suffering.

For the events, or perhaps better described as non-events of the hours and days succeeding my meeting with Amy could at least, if I had tried, have been understood and described by me to her family, fiancé and friends. There was no need for me, as I see now – and indeed saw shortly after the 'Castle Azeby wedding fiasco' (as the *Daily Express* had it) – to conceal my knowledge of what was going on. Loyalty to Amy, which I thought then inspired my silence and secrecy, was probably hardly the motive at all; rather, a jumble of mixed emotions on my part: some jealousy (of Candida in her role as favoured guest, whereas I, now asked for help and support, was to be farmed out with 'the odious Cleggs', as Ethel, for

121

some reason certain that Mrs Clegg had been at school with her in the early mists of time, insisted on calling them); some loyalty certainly; and, too, a sense that Ludo might approve of my actions, my Pimpernel streak.

For all that, what I did was wrong, and can more easily be blamed on my fatal incapacity for action when it is needed: a conviction, if that is not too strong a word, that I count for so little in myself that any word or action on my part will automatically go unheard and unseen; and that I am, in short, a recorder and listener, not a doer, and that those whose actions I record should get on with their actions perfectly well without my interference. My assistance to Amy was all in a negative capacity, then; and I felt sure she would act as was right – though this, of course, was what she wanted to run away from.

Matters to do with Amy's 'love life' (though this terminology only brought a groan or dry laugh from her) were obviously taboo. And we had got no further than an exchange of inane remarks when Daniel Stringer, the sixteen-year-old son of Wolfgang and Bettina, came over the road and prised us from the café where we were sitting, consuming coffee that in no way resembled the 'mocca' so fashionable in those days at selected West End venues. Amy, in fact, had just laid down her spoon and let out a further groan, this somehow tying in the impossibility of life and the appalling standard of the coffee in one metaphysical exclamation. There was little time to ponder this, however, for Amy's next words removed me briskly from my picturing of her coming married life – by now, in view of her obvious exhaustion, in the bedroom Candida had described to me in our schooldays, glimpsed on a long-coveted visit to Castle Azeby. ('A sort of fairy princess's four-poster – and she has a fire in her room lit every morning by a *maid*, can you believe it?') Amy's words filled the narrow, stately bed with two sad figures and as quickly emptied it again.

'I can't go through with it,' Amy said.

This was said quickly, as Daniel Stringer, sent to fetch us by Aunt Babs (who, not averse to twitching a lace curtain, had probably spotted us from the ground-floor window when we arrived), could be seen to be crossing the road and making for the café. In the few seconds remaining of my and Amy's privacy I tried to banish strong childhood memories of Aunt Babs telling me, on a visit to Rome where the Stringers lived, that Bettina, David's mother, had been formally betrothed to an Italian count when she was a girl and failed to turn up at the church. Pictures of white blossoms, trampled under foot, lilies wilting at the altar, and crowds of hatted people breathing out their impatience and anxiety like a sick incense in the church had haunted my mind for a long time – and returned to do so now, Amy's non-appearance at Azeby kirk being as terrifying and un-thinkable an absence as a page gutted from an ancient illuminated book.

At the same time – and here Daniel Stringer did enter the café – I couldn't help feeling that Amy's decision, or non-decision, was unsurprising in the circumstances. It wasn't just that Crispin Hare, 'clearly no Lothario', as Ethel had cruelly remarked on seeing the engagement photo in a copy of *Country Life*, was far from an exciting prospect for a young girl. Nor that Crispin, with, as Lord Lovescombe's bitingly sarcastic sister Amalia Drifton had remarked all those years ago at Lovegrove, 'so *little* money', would be hard pushed to provide Amy with any 'treats' – as the Lovescombes and their kind described life's little pleasures. It wasn't just that anyway: I think we all knew that we were at some kind of crossroads in those years – or by 'all' perhaps I mean especially young women – for Amy, like the rest of us, could see the possibility of an interesting life, a life more interesting and independent than that led by her mother's generation – and saw herself offered only the option of a conventional marriage, childbearing and, if her father was generous to her, continued shopping and travels abroad. She had herself chosen this, one could say, by failing to consider university – unlike Candida – but that that one mistake should consign her to a dead end had obviously become only too clear to her. I also was aware of the difficulties in finding a 'real' life and career (Aunt Babs frequently warned me against considering an early marriage and dependence on a husband). For all the gruesome mirth associated with the subject of marriage and women, particularly in that epoch, I did, as I say, understand Amy's position very clearly. Only, as it is saddening to admit even at a great span of time, the social difficulty (was it for me to tell her parents? Amy seemed a good deal too tired and upset to move another inch: was it for me to warn the minister, as I believed clerics in the north were called, of her non-attendance?) stopped me from showing immediately the full extent of my sympathy and understanding.

'Oh, Amy, that's terrible,' I said. 'What are you going to do?'

'I could stay with you and look for a job,' Amy said.

'We could share a flat, couldn't we, Jenny?' And, as Daniel Stringer finally made his way to our table and stood over us like an avenging angel – his red hair shining in the overhead fluorescent lighting – she burst into tears; and as I knew not for the first time that day. 'Help me, Jenny.' She laid a hand which was flushed and clammy to the touch on mine. 'Please.'

CHAPTER EIGHT

Memories of Aunt Babs' evening, after that, tend to run into one another, as if the stolen linen napkins, quickly plundered from the Harrods carrier-bag by Amy and used for wiping away her tears as they fell, had been procured in the first place only for this purpose: the mopping up of the years of Amy's unhappiness and uncertainty; witnesses, too, of the kindness and indifference to Amy's plight of the various people who came through Aunt Babs' house that night, and of my own cowardice and indecision, as I stood guard over what could be seen either as a refugee or a hostage – a bride absconding on her wedding eve.

To my horror, the Brigadier was the first to greet Amy as she came into our house – or 'stepped over the threshold of our humble home' as the Brigadier, despite the fact that the house belonged to my aunt and was in no way his, boomingly described the act of entry. I would have preferred, I thought, for the Stringers, eccentric though they might seem to her, to be the first of my aunt's guests to meet Amy's eye: instead, and with an inevitability reminiscent of the heath scene in *Macbeth*,

Ethel now came sharply out of the kitchen at the back of the house and looked at Amy with the kind of avid pleasure at that time reserved for only a few in the land, the days of pop stardom and mega-media events still far off on the horizon.

'Amy Rudd!' Ethel contrived both to push and pull us into the 'through' room where my aunt, in the midst of a chaos that resembled her most disastrous efforts at Christmas, was trying to arrange chrysanthemums in a frosted glass vase either too short or too tall to receive them, while at the same time laying a table with forks, spoons and small bone-handled knives for the rolls and butter.

'Isn't it your wedding very soon?' My aunt took the napkins from me absent-mindedly and without thanks, as if the finding of them had been as simple as a trip to the corner shop for groceries. She pulled out a bundle, and frowned in a preoccupied way at them before pronouncing that they were 'a bit too heavy' to hold in one hand, a plate necessarily balanced in the other. 'They're damask,' my aunt continued, in a tone which I recognized – and didn't like any the more for that – as her tone of impending doom, this coming into use invariably just before a social occasion (and, it must be said, warranted on a social occasion such as this one, where Lady Pickering, of whom Aunt Babs disapproved in the normal run of business, had to be invited by reason of her fund-raising capacities). It occurred to me that my aunt, at moments like these, would gladly abandon her children's opera, if it weren't for her idealistic – 'utopian' in the Brigadier's opinion – vision of a perfectly integrated society, the black and other immigrant children getting the chance in this way to work with the children of the long-term residents of Notting Hill. (Again, that this proved, at the time of the race riots a year later, to have been less efficacious than she would have expected, did not deter my aunt from her yearly charity work and the agonizing 'funding' dinner, with its burnt canapés and unsuitable rice dishes.)

Later I wondered at the similarity of approach to Lady Pickering from people as different as Aunt Babs and Carmen, whose approach was unfortunately little different to that taken when impersonating the poor woman at St Peter's – and to wonder, too, at what it was in this rich, frail woman that excited so great a contempt. There was a gulf, certainly between her and the rest of the human race – or so her minuscule, dainty, fur-laden person seemed to suggest; but whether this was due to South African origins and an Irish stately home – called Scudamore, the same name as the road in which Aunt Babs' house was situated, a coincidence soon exhausted in conversation after Lady Pickering's arrival at one of these charity events – or simply a physical mistrust of so simian and exquisitely groomed a creature, it would be difficult to say. Just after Amy had walked into the room – 'Welcome to our Shoebox!' the Brigadier unstoppably yelled – came Lady Pickering, whose pantry at Scudamore, as the Brigadier was fond of remarking, could swallow up my aunt's room without noticing it.

In a quite unexpected way, the worst that could happen – for I feared that Amy might blurt out her intentions not to marry Crispin at the crucial moment of canapé-handing and hand-shaking, a double feat at which Aunt Babs was far from proficient – was averted. This was due to Daniel Stringer, entering with a sudden bound, his parents in tow and beaming proudly at their prodigy, an entrance, certainly (as far as I knew) not planned by the Stringers in advance with my aunt.

Daniel's leaping, almost balletic arrival served to deflect concentration from what was actually happening in Aunt Babs' 'through' room. This was in the main the surprised reaction of Lady Pickering to her virtually unwelcomed state (the Brigadier, in her eyes, clearly counting for as little as a toastmaster with whom she was expected, quite unacceptably, to spend the rest of the evening, after being announced). This evident surprise was compounded by the sudden ingress of a sizeable number of uninvited guests.

Roly Marr was in the lead, and was followed, as I could hardly believe I saw, by Carmen and the painter Bernard Ehrlich, Candida Tarn and her brother Leo and a West Indian woman, Gloria, who was a friend, I knew, of both Roly and Ehrlich, a possible link between them having been forged by Colin MacInnes, or so rumour went in the market on an especially buzzing Saturday. Gloria was arm-in-arm this time, however, with a tall, fair-haired man, invisible at first because surrounded by a newly arrived group of children's opera organizers, their expressions baffled at finding Aunt Babs' humble fund-raising evening to have been taken over by a new 'smart set'. That the place had also been transformed into a nightclub seemed also beyond question, as the blond man's hand went out to the switch and turned off the overhead light, leaving us with a dim selection of Aunt Babs' lamps.

It was only then, as the guests stood back in mild fear at the sudden near-darkness, that it was possible to see

129

the extinguisher to be none other than Mick Scupper. Behind him, with a face of permanent bland party-going stood Charles Edge – and, doubtless, somewhere down by his penultimate rib stood Lucy Edge, whose party smile did indeed shortly reveal itself as the cortège moved further into the room. All that was needed now, I thought, was the arrival of Lord Lovescombe – perhaps to search for his daughter after hearing somehow or other that the wedding was off – and indeed Amy's father could now be seen pressing into the crush by the door, while the Brigadier's welcome, stuck by now at 'Welcome to our humble abode', stopped short at the sight of Lord Lovescombe as he appeared amongst us that night in the flesh.

This could not have been said to be a pretty sight. The coil of hair wound like a wool-card round the peer's cranium had become detached and flapped gently as he nodded and shook his head. A resemblance to a joint of meat, just untied and ready for carving, came irresistibly to mind. I remembered, indeed, the last, calamitous lunch – or 'luncheon', as Lady Lovescombe insisted on calling it, at Lovegrove – and the brave efforts made by Amy's father to cut the beef on a card table, all the majestic trestles, sideboards and so on having been, presumably, deemed for one reason or another unsuitable.

It wasn't possible – or desirable anyway – to dwell long on such memories, the sight of Nagra Pont in Amy's father's wake serving as a sharp reminder that we were in the present and not in the days of Jasmine Tremlett, by now as remote as Louise de la Vallière must have seemed to Louis XIV when he was the companion of Madame de Maintenon. Nor, of course, could it be said that Nagra Pont, with her vacant, staring gaze, long 'drowned' hair and general air of submarine intelligence, resembled that starry pedagogue, the last mistress of the *Roi Soleil*; but these thoughts, once more, were overturned by the increasingly 'glaringly obvious' – as Ethel put it when she fought her way through the crowd towards me – absence of Amy. Amy had had plenty of time to feel alienated by the proceedings and to decide to go. She had doubtless seen her father; her old schoolfriend Candida; the lover they (supposedly) shared between them, Mick Scupper; as well as a cast not unconnected with her present, her past – and thus with a totally unacceptable future.

Carmen's presence suggested strongly that this surge of guests on the eve of Amy's abstention from the matrimonial state had been set up by her. Amy must by then have wished she had never confided in Carmen; and indeed it was hard to think of a more undesirable confidante, the mixture of lies and half-truths spewed out by her old school-mate having provided in all likelihood a muddled picture of Amy as a young woman split between two men – Mick Scupper and Crispin Hare – and on the brink of fleeing from both. The other side of the story was that she was possibly bearing – or not bearing, as a result of Carmen's inevitably dangerous and unsavoury back-street advice – a child that was not Crispin's on her way up the aisle. There was little wonder, given the different versions Carmen was inclined to give out to different people, that views of Amy differed so drastically; but there was equally little wonder at our new refugee having 'fled the coop' (as the Brigadier bellowed to Lord Lovescombe, when he asked where his daughter might be). Most of the gate-crashers had come here to see a bride-to-be or a jilter – or an expectant mother, depending on the story dealt out to them.

CHAPTER NINE

Candida's eyes fixed on me as I struggled to leave the room and go in search of Amy. Apart from my urgent need to find her, I had no further wish to be, as Ethel put it later, 'entangled with' anyone there. (Indeed, both poor Aunt Babs and her friend, in their mortification at the lack of glasses and food for the influx of uninvited guests, clearly blamed me for getting them entangled in this undesirable 'set' in the first place.)

I couldn't tell them, as we sat the next day in a perfunctorily cleaned sitting-room, which bore the marks of Carmen's glass of red wine on the bobble paper – this considered the most satisfactory way of concealing cracks and other structural faults in houses in areas such as ours – that things much worse were going to happen (or, indeed, not happen, in the case of Amy's wedding) than they could possibly suspect: that the insult to Lady Pickering, who, after making 'a harmless remark to Carmen about recognizing her from a visit to St Peter's', followed by instant receipt in her face of the contents of a glass of the Beaujolais supplied by the wine society to which the Brigadier belonged, was not, either, the most alarming

133

or horrendous event of the preceding evening, as far as I was concerned.

The party had certainly not raised any funds for the local opera, though, as the Brigadier nauseatingly pointed out, it had probably gone a long way towards raising the tone of the neighbourhood, many of the residents of which would have been unlikely to have met a 'peer of the realm', as the Brigadier, endlessly exhilarated by his brief encounter with Lord Lovescombe, insisted on calling him. This, and the incident of the wine-throwing, was enough to plunge Aunt Babs and Ethel in an apparently unshakable gloom. It would have been wrong of me, I knew, to refer to the near-certainty of another débâcle – only on a much larger scale – looming in the immediate future. The absconding of the bride at her Castle Azeby wedding, while being nothing whatever to do with them, might have been enough to finish off both elderly women at one go. So I desisted from telling them any of this on the grey day which succeeded my aunt's attempt to bring harmony to the *quartier* (thus delineated by Roly Marr, who was to insist over the next twenty-five years that he had been the one to 'discover' Notting Hill and its environs).

Ethel asked me what I was going to wear to the wedding. I replied that Candida had lent me a dress which had once belonged to her mother. I was inspired in this, I suppose, by sudden memories of our dressing-up before setting off for another Lovescombe occasion, Ludo's eighteenth birthday dance, at the never-attained house in Regent's Park.

Once I had quietened Ethel's fears as to my sartorial performance the following day in Cumberland, I had the opportunity, if only for the space of half an hour before the Stringers pressed me into cultural action once more with requests for theatre tickets, timetables for the Little Venice barge trip and other London delights, to digest the evening and its implications for the future. For the question was whether I should go and warn the Loves-combes, preparing at this minute, presumably, for their journey north, that the wedding was off – or not.

Before adding up the pros and cons of this disagreeable quandary, I was forced back to the previous evening in greater detail – as if, perhaps, the actions of the uninvited and unashamed guests could help me in my agonizing decision.

I'd got as far as half-way to the door, I think, when Candida signalled to me again, this time with a greater firmness of purpose. I skirted Roly Marr and his West Indian friend Gloria in an attempt to evade her and explore the house for Amy; though something in me knew Amy was gone and had no intention of coming back either. Roly Marr tugged at my dress as I went and I had to stop. Candida's face now loomed closer, with Mick Scupper just behind.

I had to admit to myself that for a brief minute I hoped I had been wrong about Ludo and Candida. I hoped against hope that her old romance with Scupper, the cause of a long rift between herself and Amy, had now reawoken and was the cause of her indubitable air of impending matrimony. This was reinforced by the sight of Candida's fourth finger, on which a diamond and sapphire ring sparkled, while round her neck, which was later, in the same lowly tabloids perused sur-reptitiously by the Brigadier and Ethel, to be described

135

as 'swan-like', hung a strand of pearls with an equally large diamond and sapphire clasp. The pearls exactly resembled Candida, by being small and resolute in appearance, like the small but determined milk teeth of a child.

Roly Marr, who seldom missed a trick when what he would call 'a bit of gear' made itself evident in the vicinity, reached out to pull at Candida's dress as well as mine, so that we were joined suddenly like Siamese twins. Scupper was now faced with the back of Candida's slender neck and shoulders – these further enhanced by the 'boneless, strapless wonder' of her dress (as Ethel rather dismissively, in her loosish silks from the stall further up the Portobello Road, was later to describe it).

'How about that, then? Don't I recognize it?' Roly, whose encyclopaedic knowledge of all *bibelots, objets de vertu* and the rest of it had in the past resulted in short visits to Borstal (the hope among his vast number of friends and acquaintances being that a more adult institution would not be the next to be favoured by his presence) now tugged in a manner that was both friendly and familiar at Candida's fourth finger and released the gem. Gloria, at his side, gave a little squeal.

'You probably do!' Candida said. She looked down at Roly – reassuring perhaps as a ring-remover because of his expertise. Possibly, too, she was charmed by his manner, which was both queenly and ludicrous, so that I could hear Carmen, who had inevitably been drawn to our circle, give a loud snort of laughter.

'Let's have a see,' said Gloria.

'Mmm,' was Roly's reply, as, like a conjuror he slipped the ring on to Gloria's plump, black finger. Then, destroying my hope, 'From the Lovescombe collection, if I may remind you of something you already know.'

'Indeed!' Candida's resemblance to Queen Mary, then still a symbol of regal plundering, was so remarked that, catching Carmen's eye, I found myself bursting out laughing as well. It seemed all at once that I had only to lose myself, like Amy, and go out in the real world outside, to be saved for the rest of my life from the pretentiousness and cupidity of the guests at Aunt Babs' – or those, at least, who had invited themselves that evening.

'Midnight sapphire,' Roly went on in a teasing voice, as we all stared down at the dark blue of the ring and the flashing white surround on Gloria's velvety skin. 'Not for you, though, Gloria dear. Off it comes before we get too attached to it!'

Gloria, well used to admiration and attention, gave a pout, followed by a smile more dazzling than the diamonds, indicating that she, like the rest of us, possessed the certain knowledge that, even in supposedly civilized circumstances no eye would leave the valuable cluster while it circulated so promiscuously. In every mind, perhaps, there was a sudden fusing of the lights, a shout of 'Stop! Thief!', and feet running as fast as hurricane-swept leaves in the street outside.

'Amy asked me to meet her later tonight at the Sunset Club,' Gloria then announced to the assembled company.

In the confusion which followed this statement, I was aware of Candida, too far away to have heard Gloria's announcement, resuming her signalling movements; and, with Carmen now close on her heels and Mick Scupper for a reason which at that time seemed unfathomable, climbing up on a chair, very little stood between us to prevent the head-on meeting she so clearly desired. Congratulations, I decided, were what Candida was determined to wring out of me – and, near as I was to Gloria and the sapphire ring, I made up my mind with a renewed grimness that I would rather snatch the gem than extend my good wishes to the future bride of Ludo. There was a sense, too, of an appalling *déjà vu* as Candida held aloft a square of cardboard clearly depicting Castle Azeby and its environs, a scene I remembered well from the last minutes of my visit to Lovegrove, when an oil of the portals, park and children of that northern keep was displayed just before the final, larval rush of Lady Lovescombe's anger and our expulsion from the southern part of the family's estates.

'My wedding present to Amy and Crispin. Don't you think they're sweet?' Candida had 'got her way', as the form mistress used sourly to put it at St Peter's, and was now standing close to me, the deceptive fragility of her features and porcelain-blue eyes contrasting uneasily (to my mind at least) with a jaw which, as the Brigadier remarked after first meeting her, 'could swallow a billiard ball'. I saw, too, that the view of Castle Azeby was only one of a collection of such views, which were ruffled in front of me as if, in the unlikely event of my being allowed to choose a part for myself of the land in which Castle Azeby was situated, I could make up my mind there and then to select a garden of topiary chess pieces, or a waterfall garden bordered with azaleas and rhododendrons.

'Table mats,' Candida explained, as if I, and certainly my Aunt Babs, would very probably be unacquainted with such refinements, a point of view which could, I suppose, be justified on the grounds that there had been no napkins in evidence all evening, Amy having vented her misery on the whole ransacked pile by blowing her nose once on each and then tossing it into the corner. (This, as Candida would have been the first to point out, was yet another of the unmistakable signs that Amy's upbringing was as far removed from an 'ordinary' one as a cannibal's from that of a Methodist missionary, for someone else would be expected to pick them up and wash them for her.) 'Walter Neet painted them,' Candida added unnecessarily. 'I must say, I think they've come out very well.'

Before I could conclude that a part of Amy's great unhappiness came very probably from her removal on marriage from the childhood homes she doubtless loved as much as her brother – and the subsequent ownership of all these precious views by none other than Candida – a roar broke out in the room, this turning out to be both a request, in an assumed toastmaster's voice, for 'Silence, Ladies and Gentlemen, Please' and the ensuing hubbub of refusal to comply with such a request, the drink consumed having by now begun to take its toll.

'To the bride,' bellowed Scupper, holding aloft an empty champagne glass (I had seen that some of the 'nobs', as Ethel put it, had brought their own 'bubbly' – according to Carmen this time, who had all evening been brandishing a bottle of Pol Roger) and drunker than he had at first appeared; 'To dear Amy, wherever she may be.'

The toast, as was generally agreed the next morning by Ethel and my Aunt Babs, definitely 'put the cat among the pigeons'. Before resumed shouting broke out – for, almost sinisterly, an absolute silence had followed Scupper's second plea for it – it was possible to see Lord Lovescombe's face grow distinctly pale at the confirmation that his daughter was no longer there. Whether he guessed at that moment that the chances of the wedding taking place were every moment declining was of course impossible to know. For myself, I felt only an increased sense of responsibility and anxiety, for surely I should ask Gloria where Amy had arranged to meet her – if meeting they actually were – and lead father in the direction of daughter, so that he would, in the fullness of time, be able to 'give her away'. (Whether my aunt's early association with Dora Russell and the other libertarian and feminist principles espoused by her in her youth in the Camden School did in some way prevent me from doing this I shall, again, never know.)

Gloria, however, had disappeared when I came to look for her; and the ring was back on Candida's finger, presumably returned while I had been staring up at Scupper's flushed and offended face (would he, I wondered, rush into the little Castle Azeby church and declare an impediment to the wedding of the cousins, and if so, what would he do on discovering, after expending so considerable an effort, that the groom stood alone, Scupper's intervention appearing more like an effort to marry at all costs into the Azeby family than to assert his undying fidelity to Amy?). In the crush of now-departing guests – Lady Pickering bewilderedly among them – I lost Lord Lovescombe as well; and it was only as I made my way to the furthest part of the room from my aunt, whose indignation at the gate-crashing numbers and general arrogance of what Roly Marr was fond of calling the *gratin* was beginning to make itself palpable (myself,

I feared, as the main target for her rage, as introducer of this impossible 'bunch of philistines') that Candida once more caught up with me and tugged at my arm with a thoroughness I recognized from the days of the lacrosse team, when to beat her was to receive a grip very similar to this.

'Amy is at my house,' Candida mouthed at me over the sounds of a departing and discontented horde. She shook her head impatiently when I called back that I thought Amy was at a club, famed for its music and violence, up the road. 'No, no, she's in no state for that.' (This, I must say, was certainly true.) 'Come back with me, Jenny, and see her. She wanted a little breather, I think, before the big event.'

CHAPTER TEN

Some people, as was impressed on me as a child by my aunt and others, never grow up – and it is this thought, still bringing the unease and grief inevitably connected with such a state of permanent immaturity, that returns to haunt me when I relive those hours spent in pursuit of Amy; and when I think of their inevitable result. I could have compared myself to some kind of sprite at the time, had it occurred to me to do so, for Aunt Babs, still as much an Edwardian in her own way as the Lovescombes were in theirs, was fond of quoting Barrie (and, on occasions, of threatening to build a 'Wendy House' in the thin, urban patch of grass behind our house). But I felt, I think, more like the mistletoe which Candida had described to me in awestruck terms as hanging from the Druidic oaks in the northern forests of Castle Azeby, and which she had seen on a Christmas stay before I had known either her or Amy.

I was a parasite, I thought, living off the emotions, loves and disappointments of others; and if, on my flying visit to the Tarns' later that evening and later when tempted by Carmen to go and seek her in the Mandrake Club at cock's crow – I was filled with any genuine feelings of my own, they seemed by now to be inextricably intertwined with those of the Lovescombes, so that it was no longer feasible to divide them and to stand on my own. That the host body would, as had happened at the time of the visit to Lovegrove, reject me once more, I was sure, for I was rootless, never, in the terms of the Lovescombes, having sprung from the ground in any recognizable way; and yet, having known this for many years and made my life as an apprentice gilder, as a dweller in the studios and attics still rank with the paint and turpentine smells of my aunt's art-student past, I was, as I think now, subtly poisoned while I hung there in my hopeless attachment to both sister and brother.

In its profound desire to discourage what Amalia Drifton, Lord Lovescombe's sister, had with a short laugh referred to as 'hangers-on', the head office – as it were – of the Lovescombes and Azebys emitted a strong but subtle signal, the effect of which would bring on a slumbrous illness, a sense of malaise, a state of total dangerous dependence. The result of this, of course, was the increased inability of the 'leech' (the Brigadier's name for any visitor to my aunt's house who stayed longer than an hour or drank more than two glasses of his wine club selection) to move away from the main support at all. I was no more than a permanent scrounge, I had to conclude very sorrowfully as I set off after my aunt's soon-to-be notorious party ('Mystery of the Missing Bride' was the next day's *Express* headline, causing my poor aunt, with her pronounced ambiguous attitude to publicity, almost to have a breakdown) in search of what had once been a friend at school and could not now be described

143

as 'close', so long had been Amy's absences and silences.

It seemed to me, which is hardly a defence, that I was forced by some power beyond myself to find Amy; and that the blue ring on Candida's finger was the stone which drew me, finally, to her house that night. The time had come, too, for the truth to come from Candida's lips. She was going to marry Ludo; and soon; and that was the end of it.

The enormous amount of inconvenience, not to say damage, which succeeded Amy's visit that night to my aunt's should have persuaded me to forget these sentiments and help clear up the mess, both physical and psychological, which Amy's casually chosen haven now suffered. That I chose instead to 'fly off', as my aunt, in a distinctly chilly manner, phrased it, showed only my continued refusal to face reality.

CHAPTER ELEVEN

The Tarns' house was much as it had been in the days when I was at school with Candida, the main difference being the replacement of the brown linoleum so pervasive in those days by a hallful of electric blue carpet, the colour and upwardly ascending and similarly carpeted staircase suggesting the recent edict of the Prime Minister Harold Macmillan that we 'had never had it so good'. This impression was cancelled, however, by the frowning face of Mrs Tarn, a frown which indicated that things of the mind were of far greater importance than mere decoration of the home and that the search for a discontented heiress on the eve of her wedding to a young executive of less significance even than that.

It was clear also, from the start, that Amy, despite Candida's claim that she was taking some sort of breather before the surrendering of her name and assumed purity, was not at present at the Tarns', the only reminder of her being a pile of Castle Azeby place mats, presented presumably to her mother by Candida on the eve of her own triumphant conjunction with the house of Lovescombe.

145

I had to look away from the over-familiar view, as depicted by Walter Neet, of the gatehouse at Castle Azeby, with brother and sister mysteriously and permanently together in the porch, as if the heavy layer of varnish applied to these already 'reproduction' items of Harrods tableware had fixed their childhood alliance for ever. As I did so, Leopold Tarn came heavily down the stairs and into the kitchen: sounds of a kettle being filled ensued, and drawers opening and shutting angrily.

'The demo has been a big strain,' Mrs Tarn announced, glad perhaps to be returned to a world where the bomb posed more of a threat to mankind than the postponed or cancelled wedding of the scions of an industrial and recently ennobled family whose fortunes had, as she must certainly have known, been overtaken by superior German efficiency at least half a century before. 'Ah. Now this gives me some problems,' Mrs Tarn added with an even greater note of relief, as a gliding figure reached the electric blue of the hall and disappeared like a ghost into the kitchen, the door closing soundlessly behind it. 'We have no vegetable curry in the house.'

The suppression of laughter, childish as it always is, brought on, however, nothing more than a further surge of longing to return to the everlasting nursery, where Ludo, Amy and I could play at grown-ups without the responsibility the actual condition must bring; and Candida, possibly picking some of this up, spoke next in a tart and recognizably governessy tone.

'Amy must have slipped away somewhere. It's very silly of her to have late nights just before her wedding. Jenny, did you say she asked if she could stay with you?'

Candida's Wedgwood-blue eyes looked at me disbelievingly, as if, having witnessed my aunt's domestic arrangements that evening, and the manifest lack of available china and cutlery at the 'fund-raising party', she would find it hard to give credence to Amy's wish to spend the night with us; or, if she did, of there being so much as a camp bed to sleep on. I told her that this was indeed the case; and went on to say that Amy had decided not to go through with her marriage; that she had asked to stay with us until she could find somewhere permanent for herself; and that I hadn't really believed that she had gone to the Tarns', though Candida's seeming total knowledge of all Lovescombe intentions and movements had taken me in for a short time and I had agreed to come along.

'She asked to stay here.' Candida's eyes flashed, my attack of spite having registered visibly and a careful revenge already plotted, as the lowered jaw and mutinous expression only too clearly showed. 'I never heard such rubbish, Jenny. Amy *has* to get married. She's expecting a child!'

As so often happens on occasions when a fact, long unacknowledged – in this case discredited by Carmen's insistence on it – is brought brutally out into the open, I was aware both of a sense of shock and familiarity. Returned to childhood as I was by my fatal conjunction with the Lovescombe family, I thought involuntarily of the 'thunder and lightning' puddings given to me by my aunt when I was small, golden syrup and cream when poured over suet giving the same almost frightening feeling of two conflicting and temporarily conjoining worlds. Bodily heat was followed by cold at this news – and followed again by a strong sense of relief, that as Amy

147

'had to get married' I would most certainly not have to go on worrying about her. This, in turn, though interrupted by Mrs Tarn's growl of disapproval and the door, opening to the kitchen, revealing Leo and his friend coming out with mugs of some steaming hot drink in their hands, was rapidly succeeded by the realization that Candida's information was not necessarily the gospel, as far as Amy was concerned. The wedding night could just as well not take place, whether Amy was pregnant or not. My own responsibilities in the matter, far from being diminished, increased sharply as I contemplated them. Candida, whose wearing of the sapphire ring, as I had just had time to notice, had attracted no comment from her mother – and was thus, presumably, an accepted fact of the Tarn household – must have entertained similar thoughts, possibly as a future sister-in-law to a disgraced member of the family, bearer of a child without a name and thus dragging her own into the mire – and for the first time looked worried and uncertain. 'Look, Jenny, she must have said something to you. About where she was really going, I mean. We must save Amy. We must!'

'My sister wishes to save the ruling class,' Leo said, stepping into the brightly lit passage and gesticulating with his mug, so that another groan escaped from Mrs Tarn at the slopping of cocoa on to the expanse of royal blue. 'That, in my house, you did not expect to find!'

Before there was time to wonder whether Leo's Germanic turn of phrase was part of some inheritance from his parents which he was determined to cultivate, or the result of a too-prolonged reading of *The Grundrisse*, the phone had given out what appeared to be a particularly jangling ring. Mrs Tarn cried to God in alarm and anger at the sound, and Candida, with her customary presence of mind, went to the hall to answer it. She held the receiver close to her ear for a time calculated to bring further annoyance to both members of her family present; then, just as the Indian guest was attempting to slip up the stairs to renewed safety, she barked out an affirmative and slammed the already frail-looking instrument back in its cradle.

'That was Carmen. She says Amy has just left the Mandrake and gone to the Gargoyle.' Candida paused – for as long as her sense of theatre would permit her – to show signs of disapproval at being forced to utter the names of these *louche* (Bettina Stringer's way of describing low life to such as myself) establishments. 'If we go there at once we'll find her. Carmen is going to stay with her until we come.'

CHAPTER TWELVE

In retrospect, the alarming odyssey on which I was now forced to embark seems almost comic, the crashing storms and shipwrecks of the nightclub visits being succeeded by the deadly calm of anti-climax.

At the Gargoyle (at that epoch, according to the band of drunken revellers Walter Neet, J. D. Hare and their bunch of cronies, 'on its last legs') artificial stars let into the ceiling gave out a baleful and dim light. This turned Candida, with her pale hair and Teutonic features, into a threatening, even dangerous figure, a *femme fatale* as painted by the Expressionists; or even, as Victor Crane raised himself from a prone position under a far table and pointed dramatically at her, Circe encircled by her swine. That there was no sign of Amy was soon manifestly clear, despite the gloom; but that Carmen, companion to those patrons incapacitated by the amount of alcohol they had consumed ('hooch', as the Brigadier insisted on remarking at this point in the tale) *was* there was equally clear, the sound of breaking glass from the table occupied by J. D. Hare giving audible proof of her presence.

150

'Christ!' Candida muttered, her face showing for the first time in my knowledge of her a look of uncertainty and fear almost akin to the Munch reproduction of *The Scream* on the walls of her mother's dining-room. 'Come on Jenny, let's run. Amy's not here, and quite honestly I don't want to see Carmen at all.'

A residue of prim, slightly lisping reasonableness in Candida's tone allayed my fears slightly – foolishly, as I was soon to discover. It seemed to me then, in this highly unpalatable setting, where smashed bottles rolled from banquettes upholstered in a rubbed velvet only describable as the colour of sweat, with a painted night sky apparently about to come down on us all, crowning us with tinsel stars, that the expression on Candida's face betrayed moral disapproval, even disgust; and, for once, despite frequent accusations on the part of Ethel of my wishing to 'go to Soho for a bit of *nostalgie de la boue*', I agreed with her; without realizing – as indeed, how could I? – the real reason for her horror and disapprobation. The voice – so reminiscent of the schoolrooms and gyms of my long and deadly vigil at St Peter's – seemed in this *milieu* quite reassuring: even the spectre of Lord Lovescombe, tie askew and lipstick-cheeked – and now bearing down on us – was a minor irregularity with which she, clearly marked out as one of Nature's Head Girls, could easily cope. If her look of consternation was in some way allied to the unpleasant spectacle of a man in his cups – 'drunk as a lord', as the Brigadier was to comment with some relish – then this was hardly surprising, given that Candida had, as I had every reason also to conclude, the expectation of having him as a father-in-law. That the wedding of Amy, to be expedited as

151

efficiently as possible, was now possibly off can hardly have pleased or assuaged her, the sight of the bride's father manifestly in no condition to horsewhip his daughter – metaphorically of course – indicating a lack of control just where control was most needed. Carmen's hanging on to the arm of Lord Lovescombe, a position just taken up in one bound across the small circular dance-floor, prodded Candida to further unusual and, to her, 'unladylike' mobility.

'It's too much,' is all she would say as we raced down the steep stairs, the snail's crawl of the tiny lift being clearly unacceptable in the circumstances. 'We *must* find Amy. This can't go on.' And, suddenly like some fleeing, tumbling Alice as depicted by Tenniel, grabbing my hand as we hurtled down the last flights and out into a quiet, dark malodorous Soho street, 'There's only one other place we can look for her, Jenny. Are you coming with me? At home!'

Home was not, I must confess, the first place I would have thought of looking for a bride who had no intention of going through with her wedding. That I hadn't told Candida of Amy's defection earlier was, I realized then, responsible for the assumption that she had decided to go to ground – or had conceivably 'taken leave of her senses' (the Brigadier) on the ensuing morning, when I had to own up too late to my aunt that I had had a strong suspicion all along as to the whereabouts of the 'Lovescombe heiress'. Her disappearance was already a feature in the *Express* of the day, the snippet provided presumably by Mick Scupper, first to notice the absence of the bride at Aunt Babs' party and the first to publicize it, whether or not for the dubious honour of receiving a fee of ten pounds for the service could not be ascertained. Whatever the reason, it had to be said that the outlook was bad; and my own behaviour in concealing Amy's intentions even worse. I must go and 'beard the Lovescombes in their den', as Ethel said, in fine voice on the morning after the disaster of my poor aunt's party. 'Go and tell them where she is, Jenny, for goodness' sake, if you really think you know. Go and tell them straight away before they get ready to go up to the wedding. Before they leave home!'

As I saw it, home was almost certainly where Amy was not to be found. Yet I couldn't help wondering, as I begged to be allowed to wait at least until a civilized hour before confronting the Lovescombes (I had heard from Candida that Lady Lovescombe liked to rise late; and was likely to empty her bath water, by means of a pipe the outlet of which was mysteriously positioned just above the front door of the Regent's Park house, on to the heads of guests arriving at one o'clock for lunch) whether Candida's sudden certainty as to the whereabouts of the *jeune mariée* – as Roly Marr at his most precious had liked to gloat over Amy and the coming nuptials at Castle Azeby and his own intended light-fingered visit to the reception with its concomitant treasures on display – was not, possibly, well founded.

Candida's expectation of finding her there was, I decided nevertheless, more to do with fear of not finding her there than with probability. Her greatest rival, she must have sensed, was Amy, when it came to the securing of Ludo; and no amount of sapphires round her neck or on her fingers would convince her otherwise. If Amy had decided, on the eve of marriage, to throw it all in and go

153

home, it would be a grand gesture of loyalty to her brother: an admission, too, that no husband would stand in the way of her unswerving devotion to him. And Candida must, at some meeting between the three of them in the past days, have picked up the existence of a renewed bond, perhaps expressed in laments at the soonness of the wedding and Amy's imminent departure for an undisclosed destination ('The honeymoon,' as the Brigadier declaimed with satisfaction when reading of the wedding in one of the more dignified tabloids, 'will be spent abroad'). It had taken, in fact, my announcement that I had a very strong inkling as to where Amy had disappeared to, to dissuade Candida from dragging me to Regent's Park in the middle of the night, an expedition that would have resulted in the same lack of success, I feared, as when we had set out from her home as schoolgirls to try and walk to Ludo's midsummer ball – and it was only when we had paid an equally unsuccessful visit to the Sunset Club in Notting Hill and it was demonstrably far too late to think of calling on Amy's parents and demanding if their daughter was indeed there, that Candida demanded to know what my credentials had been for taking her to this 'disgusting dive'.

'At least we're near home,' Candida added sulkily, as we climbed into the bumpy little Morris Minor shared by her and Leo (and with little amicability on either side, as far as one could make out). 'I just don't believe in this rendezvous you heard her make, Jenny. You dreamt up the whole thing because you're still sweet on Ludo and you didn't want to go to the Lovescombes' house in case he was there. Isn't that right?'

I had to hand it to Candida, as so often before, that

when it came to giving offence in the most direct manner possible there was no one to beat her. But, again as so frequently on previous occasions, I was dead tired after the successive and quite remarkable failures of the evening; I needed a lift to Portobello Road, for although we were in Notting Hill already the area was rough at night, especially in the vicinity of the Sunset, a 'spade club' much patronized by the Bohemian intelligentsia of the time (some of this species only too evidently in search of this roughness) and on top of all this my 'contact', in the shape of Roly's friend Gloria, whom I had been told Amy was planning to meet after her speedy departure from my aunt's, was clearly not in evidence. Wearily, I concluded that Amy was, after all, very probably 'at home'.

On more sober reflection the morning after – if the passage of a few hours' uneasy sleep could be called that – I was almost certain that this was the case. Yet, having felt duty-bound to describe to my aunt and Ethel the extent of the determination on Amy's part not to 'tie the knot' (the Brigadier at his most unctuous, while Aunt Babs would look away in sheer horror at the implied proposal in his tone) there was obviously still doubt over the question as to where she could be. 'Don't leave it *too* late,' Ethel said when I had explained that I had no desire to go to the Regent's Park house, but felt that I must, 'or' – and here she showed an unworldliness shared by my aunt, and, as I came to realize later, with me too: for surely a family such as the Lovescombes would, despite the 'ninety indoor servants' as related by Carmen, go north well in advance of the day? (and indeed it was only the exceptional behaviour of both the bride and her father which prevented this) – 'they might have already left, you know. Then you'd have to go up to Castle Azeby after all.'

CHAPTER THIRTEEN

In the event, Ethel's words proved only too drearily prophetic. Still the sense of *déjà vu*, as in a dream that is only a continuation of the previous one – and that merely one in a succession of horrifying visions and nocturnal visitations – led me out into the street again, without a thought of what I would do if I *did* in fact find Amy's parents placidly and happily (as far as was possible for them) preparing for a family wedding; and, with the obscure logic of dreams, I found I had taken a raincoat – an old one of my aunt's – from the stand in the hall even though it was a bright, fine day and there was no sign of rain in the offing. Like a somnambulist I crossed Portobello Road. I skirted the stall where Ethel, made late by the over-stimulating revelations of the *Daily Express* and her own not inconsiderable hangover (caused, as I was to hear later, by heavy alcohol consumption after a proposition from the Brigadier the night before, when he had suggested they go together to Paris to replenish wine supplies and also, as my aunt disgustedly informed me, to 'have a bit of oolala') would set out her mouldy wares: Walter Scott, the Waverley edition with most of the gold

157

lettering scraped off the spine; or De Quincey's *Confessions of an Opium Eater* in a condition almost indistinguishable from the pulp of old market refuse awaiting the next dustmen's carts. I wasn't surprised, surprise being normally connected with a waking state, when Carmen, so recently the vendor of the white Chelsea dove to my aunt – and now, as it appeared, the raven of the Lovescombe family bringing discord and destruction in her wake – appeared further down the market. She lifted a bunch of bananas and laid them flat on top of her head, wiggling her hips simultaneously in the 'Carmen Miranda' imitation which had been one of the factors involved in her expulsion from St Peter's years before.

'Candida's out of date,' were Carmen's words when the bananas had been retrieved by a stallholder and we strolled down in the direction of Westbourne Grove, where, I had decided, I would pay money for a taxi to take me to the Lovescombes' Regent's Park house, so late had the hour become and so paralysing the sense of helplessness in which I seemed to be caught. I had asked about Amy's pregnancy, feeling once more, I suppose, those pangs of pity for her which, combined with her own natural arrogance and my aptitude for submission, had led me so frequently into a conjunction with the family that was disastrous, if only to myself. 'You mean she's not having a baby at all?' We stood on the corner of Colville Road and looked out at a wide, taxiless expanse. Memories of Amy and Scupper on the night of her ball came back only too vividly: these, added to the extreme improbability of Crispin Hare and his cousin, as Carmen would put it, 'having it off', made the prospects for Amy's happiness, whether she went through with the marriage or not, seem bleak indeed. A taxi cruised past, but failed to pay attention to my frantic signals. Carmen glanced at me curiously. 'I told you, Candida's out of date.' Carmen's tone was menacing now, and I had no desire to examine the reason for Candida's calculations having been suddenly rendered valueless. 'Why on earth are you going to see them all, Jenny? Why don't you just drop it?'

A burst of rage, unusual for me, turned me on my heel and up against Carmen. 'They don't *know* that Amy's not going through with it,' I shouted. 'Can't you see? It would be *wrong* of me not to tell them in time –'

'In time?' Carmen gave a hoarse laugh. 'It's nothing to do with what Amy wants, old dear. The wedding was nearly going to be off, I agree. But Bluey made another offer just at the last minute and J. D. Hare agreed to sign. So now old man Lovescombe's got the whole business and he can tell Crispin exactly what to do. One of the things he's done is resell the *bijou* residence in Chelsea: too expensive, he says. Now they'll live in that mansion block on the Embankment.'

Carmen had, as usual, played a series of trump cards which, while being almost certainly tricks and *trompe-l'œil*, still retained enough verisimilitude to make the other player unsure of the next move. She laughed almost straight into my open mouth as another taxi, this time both passengerless and prepared to stop for my still-outstretched arm, chugged to a halt beside us.

'Go and see for yourself if you must,' she said – as with a faltering step (for could it be true that money was really, as Carmen would claim, the arbiter of all men's actions; and, if so, wasn't poor Amy more of a victim of an eighteenth-century type of society than even of a Victorian one?) I climbed into the cab and it set off.

'You'll miss the wedding special!' Carmen shouted after me. 'St Pancras at noon. I couldn't face Nagra's posh car. That's where I'm going!' And, as the cab went through streets which seemed to me in my state of disassociation to be lined with those who either were or were not intended to be guests at the Castle Azeby wedding, her last words floated down to me past all the shoppers and tradesmen, ignorant of the Lovescombe family drama and therefore unreal to me, that 'There'll be no one left in London, Jenny. You'll see!'

The thought that I had in some way failed Amy carried me almost blindly to Regent's Park. Children were gathering conkers, I remember that; and a red squirrel, still in its habitat in those days, ran in the square garden as we turned into the private road by the side of the park where the Lovescombes lived. Even at this length of time, I prefer not to think of those shuttered windows, blank as the reverse side of the thick white invitation cards the Lovescombes favoured; or the top nursery window, still with its bars from the nursery days, where I half expected to see Amy's face peering out. There was no sign of the Lovescombe Bentley by the kerb, where Vine would stand and wait – to take Amy to Harvey Nichols, or Lady Lovescombe to the dusty studio where she would divest herself of tweed suit, lingerie and pearls and be carnivorously portrayed by Bernard Ehrlich. It was obvious to me at last: they had gone: I should have minded my own business, kept away. But the voice nagged me still. Had they all gone north in the expectation of finding

160

Amy there, when I, the only person in the world to whom she honestly confided, knew she was never going to turn up? Was Carmen, in saying the wedding was now definitely on, telling the truth – or were her lies simply sent to tempt me into inertia, to what amounted to a betrayal of an old friendship? And wouldn't Ludo thank me if I made an already embarrassing situation, reported or at least hinted at in the press, a great deal better by preventing the long unrewarded wait in the chilly kirk, the exasperation of Lord Lovescombe and the tears of the mother of the bride? After one last look at the stony, closed face of the house in Regent's Park, I directed the cab to St Pancras station.

CHAPTER FOURTEEN

I did, of course, just miss the wedding special (and Carmen's company, a mixed blessing on a long journey); and had to board a train that seemed to take a week or so as it climbed painfully up the side of England. Worse, the dream now became banal – for it was only as we pulled slowly out of the station that I saw I was in my aunt's old raincoat and not in clothes suitable for a wedding or reception in the least. The only mercy was that I had some money on me – and a tattered copy, symbolically enough, of Rosamund Lehmann's *Dusty Answer* – for which, as may be imagined, I felt grateful in those long hours in a carriage that smelt already of abandonment: of cigarette ends and upholstery sharp with the haste of travellers; and here and there, as we came into the Satanic glow of the Midlands, of iron filings and dust.

'Walter Neet!'
I had asked the taxi from Azeby station to wait on the crest of the hill, and the voice of the elderly painter – for

such it was – took me back eerily to the first time we had met, at Lovegrove, when I was innocent still of the extraordinary damage and unhappiness the Lovescombe family could cause, not only to its own members but to anyone who happened to cross its path.

I mumbled a greeting to Neet and looked out with something approaching hatred at the purple mountains dwarfing the tiny kirk opposite us, the great waterfall in the distance where Amy had said Lord Lovescombe was prone to vanish with his mistress of the time, Jasmine Tremlett; and the towers and gargoyles of Castle Azeby itself, as delineated by Walter Neet and now encapsulated on the place mats planned as a wedding present to a parting incumbent from a future one. Neet had at least turned my nightmare into farce; and this was all, in my self-preoccupied state, I was capable of thinking, it taking Neet himself to proffer a reason for his presence at snow-level on the border with what the Brigadier insisted on calling Hibernia.

'Had some trouble with my truss.' Neet's cheeks, still clear in my memory since my last encounter as miniature puffballs communicating with each other by means of a moustache not dissimilar from the scraggy heather at our feet, blew in and out painfully. 'Just bought the damn thing so as to feel comfortable at the wedding and then it caught on a door handle before leaving.' The cheeks blew out for one last time and then subsided. 'They might have laid on a relief train, don't you think, for this kind of contingency?'

It seemed impossible to envisage a trainload of trussed wedding guests making their way north, so I asked if the wedding had actually taken place or not. Neet shrugged, probably catching the fatalistic tone in my voice. 'Your guess is as good as mine, my dear girl. I had to hitch-hike from the station, they said the only taxi was waiting for the Clegg house party. Would that be you, by any chance?'

'I suppose so.' The horror, just dawning on me, that I would be expected to join in a weekend of celebrations with the unknown Cleggs started to come home with full force. And in my raincoat, too, I thought with an almost satisfied grimness. Well, we'll see about that.

By now, Neet was waving and pointing excitedly. 'It's them! Oh, how moving!' Unexpectedly, the aged artist removed a handkerchief from a trouser pocket – presumably somewhere in the region of the offending truss, as he then let out a loud groan – and dabbed at his eyes before blowing his nose with a sound that startled the sheep straying near us. 'At least I can say I saw the bride, God bless her!' Neet went on, this time on a note more suitable for the glimpsing of Queen Victoria – or so I thought when I had time and tolerance to relive the ludicrous scene – than a modern married woman, whether a daughter of the Lovescombes or not. A glance in the direction of the kirk did indeed show, like two wooden dolls outside a Swiss chalet – one out when it is about to rain, the other when sunshine is expected – the unusual sight, in this case, of bride and groom to-gether: then, equally doll-like, the parents of the happy couple followed suit; and Mick Scupper in a white tie and tails which at this distance caused him to resemble the miniature models of bridegrooms that are sometimes, perplexingly, sold as doll's house inhabitants in shops. I thought I could make out Henry Azeby at his side, in scarlet hunting gear; and then, with a sinking heart, the blue apparition of Candida Tarn. Carmen, only too easily distinguishable in a fuchsia silk 'number' picked up at the stall a few feet down from Ethel's, stood incongruously at her side.

'Well I never!' Neet, who was making frame-like movements with his arms, recognizable to me after a lifetime with the Stringers as the movements made by a painter when planning the scope and contents of a picture, now dropped his arms to his side and made an explosive noise half-way between a belch and a whistle. His moustache, apparently alarmed by the ambiguous nature of the sound, rose up in bristles like a startled hedgehog. 'I must say I do think that's pretty blatant. Going a bit far is what I say.'

Remembering Neet's 'crush' on Carmen that summer at Lovegrove, a passion easily and rapidly eclipsed by the disappearance of Candida with Scupper into the bushes and thence to the Gothic turret in the Children's Garden, I was careful not to ask the cause of his indignation. Neet, however, was clearly determined to let me share his views. He leant very close, exuding a smell that was ineffably his, a mixture of garlic and turpentine overlaid with a sweet, spicy scent probably from Trumpers Hairdressers, an establishment he patronized in order to emulate Lord Lovescombe (or so he had once told me). On this occasion he quite clearly had other things on his mind than personal freshness, or the lack of it.

'They couldn't wait for Amy to get married, so as to announce the divorce,' Neet continued mysteriously. 'Doesn't look too savoury, does it? Although I suppose there'll be some changes made here and one might do a few little sketches for them. That's the arrangement, apparently –' Neet swivelled his head away from me and then back again. 'Lady Lovescombe's going to keep the London house. Candida and Lord L are going to be based up here. With a flat in Hill Street, of course.'

'Candida and Lord L,' I said. The words seemed to come out slowly, as if I were speaking under water; and in fact, as Neet's head waved at intervals in front of me, I might well have been trying to understand the communications of a large-headed crustacean. 'You mean that Candida and Lord Lovescombe are going to marry?'

'I thought everyone knew.' Neet was now waving impatiently at a jeep which was in the process of climbing the steep sides of the hill towards us. The taxi driver, who had also been viewing the proceedings at Azeby kirk, called out a friendly greeting. 'Can't think what poor Ludo will make of all this,' Neet said as the driver of the jeep came into view behind the wheel. 'Maybe he'll take us down there for a glass of champagne, eh there, Jenny?'

CHAPTER FIFTEEN

The rest of the events of that day are out of reach of memory, so profound were the effects of the Lovescombe family on my life at that stage in it; but I do know that we all went to the castle, and that there was a large reception where the cartwheel hats worn by the women entirely hid Amy and her new husband Crispin from view. I didn't hear Lord Lovescombe's speech because Ludo, taking me suddenly by the arm, led me up to the room which had clearly been Amy's all her girlhood – and would now be left by her for ever, tall four-poster and scarlet silk curtains and all. Ludo made me sit there; it was growing dark, although there was still some northern light coming in from the hills – and he pulled a scrap of blue satin ribbon from under the bed and handed it to me. 'Amy must have forgotten this. Silly girl!' Then he sighed. 'Don't go in for this sort of thing very much, you know, Jenny. Do you?'

I had to say I didn't. But Candida's sapphires – and engagements and marriage, the main props of a young woman's mind in those far-off days – were probably still burning away in me, for Ludo rose to his feet and said we should go down to the guests, 'or,' he said, 'it'll be cruel to Mummy.' He paused at the door as we went out and said he was off to Lagos the following day.

'But we'll have dinner when I get back, Jenny. Amy's got your number. And I'll give you a ring.'

It must have been about six months later, when I had forgotten my relief at being rescued from the wedding at Castle Azeby by Charles and Lucy Edge and driven all the way to London instead of being forced to stay with the Cleggs or undergo a further interminable train journey, that the Brigadier, making an evening call to my aunt, started to speak very much against my wishes about the Lovescombe family and what he termed their 'ramifications'. I had been in Florence on an art course and staying with the Stringers for all that time; and the mention of the name, as I recall, had only a faintly jarring effect, as if harm done in the past had at last been dispersed by study, art and good sense.

'Went to Paris,' the Brigadier said – not catching the eye, as I noticed, of my Aunt Babs nor referring to 'oolala' in any way, this latter being at least something to be thankful for. 'Must have been on her honeymoon – Amy, I mean.'

'Amy?' I said, sounding I knew like someone training to act, and unsuccessfully at that. 'And how was she? Amy, I mean?'

'Dunno, really. Little nightspot in the Place Pigalle.' The Brigadier, waiting for a shocked comment from my aunt and failing to get it, put on a brisker tone. 'She was with that husband of hers, of course. Crispin what's-his-name. But she wasn't dancing with him, I can tell you. She was dancing with a black woman – you know, Jenny, I could have sworn I'd seen her face round here – but I hardly liked to go up and say anything in case one had got the whole thing wrong. If you know what I mean.'